The cure for HIV is a death warrant for fifty million people around the world. Can Trevor stop genetics lab DNAY from releasing the toxin, or will a select few rule a devastated new world?

Introducing Special Agent Trevor Byrne

Trevor kissed her. His heart beat faster, and his breathing became shallow. He opened his eyes to make sure Lyn's were closed. His tongue entered her mouth, and she began to remove her clothes.

She slipped her jacket off, and Trevor removed his own. Lyn loosened his tie and pulled it over his head. He did the same with her chemise. He was spellbound by her barely covered, voluptuous breasts. The full, round orbs strained to free themselves from her white lace bra. Lyn moaned in response to the bulge in Trevor's pants.

Lyn unbuttoned his shirt. Trevor slid the bra's straps off her arms and brushed the cups down. She began to squirm, and he found that her skirt and panties were gone. Lyn finished undressing him then led him to the sofa and pushed him down on his back. The song playing now was his favorite Sade song, the improved version of "Never as Good as the First Time."

JOHN E. BAILOR

DEATH DEALT THE HAND

This is a work of fiction. Names, characters, places, and incidents are products of the author's imagination or are used fictitiously and are not to be construed as real. Any resemblance to actual events, locales, organizations, or persons, living or dead, is entirely coincidental.

Published by:
John E. Bailor
PO Box 684
Elizabethville, PA 17023-0684

www.johnebailor.com

ISBN: 978-0-6151-6540-0

Front cover art © 2007 by Shirley Burnett

To God,

with you all things really are possible

and

Melissa,

for the difference you've made in my life.

ACKNOWLEDGEMENTS

My first published book wouldn't have been possible without some very important people: my parents, George and Rachael Bailor. Without you none of the stories would be possible. Thanks for your corrections and suggestions.

This book is much better than my earlier efforts thanks to the terrific advice and suggestions of: David Halk, Dorissa Bolinski, Becky and Bill King, John Stanchak (author of <u>Civil War</u>), and John W. Humphrey, Jr.

A special thanks to two talented professionals who took time from their busy schedules to provide blurbs for a rookie: James Rollins and Paul Kyriazi.

More thanks to Heather Spence, Editor; M, for the photo of me; and Shirley Burnett, who created the great front cover that caught your attention.

Be sure to visit me on the web at
www.johnebailor.com

PROLOGUE

She placed the last of the three healthy monkeys inside the environmental test chamber and closed the door. They were separated from the infected subjects in the other half of the chamber by a thin transparent partition her subordinates had installed yesterday.

Marisa Menendez was the only technician on the project who knew the true purpose of Doctor Charles Garrett's testing, and that was only because he needed her assistance. If this experiment was as successful as those performed on the rats and rabbits, the healthy monkeys would remain unharmed. The two monkeys infected with HIV and the one with AIDS would die.

Everything appeared in order, so she entered the code to lock the chamber. No one would open it before the toxicity reached nil. She could only imagine the stench of decay Mel would experience if he forgot to wear an oxygen mask when he opened the chamber for disposal and sanitation.

She picked up her clipboard and checked off the final prep item. Marisa walked into the sterile control room and saw Professor Garrett making some last minute notes in his heavy handed scrawl. He turned to her. She was used to his disheveled appearance and hardly noticed the unkempt gray hair or the morning's growth of stubble. From behind the wire-rimmed glasses, his narrowed eyes locked onto hers, and she stiffened involuntarily.

The steel in the professor's voice matched that in his eyes. "Menendez, are you finished with the checklist? Are the preparations complete?"

He treated his Senior Research Technician like a rookie. She held out the clipboard, and he snatched it from her. He read over each task and stopped when he reached the bottom of the page.

"The code. You've entered the code to be sure the chamber is not opened prematurely?"

She breathed in slowly. It was exciting to be part of this breakthrough project. She'd be able to sell her story and make a fortune once the world learned about it, but first she had to stay calm and convince herself that the professor would treat anyone like this. It wasn't just her. "Yes, sir. The lock is engaged. Everything is ready when you are, professor."

The big man's voice boomed, "After two and a half years, I'm damn well ready." He adjusted his glasses and glanced once more at the checklist. Apparently satisfied, he strode to the console. "Very well."

Marisa stood next to him, so she could confirm the readouts for their records. He nodded and pressed the button. The timer began at the same moment the vapor streamed into the chamber. She looked up to observe the monkeys.

The professor had kept the sound turned off, so they did not hear the monkeys' annoying chatter. The monkeys jumped from the sudden moisture. Soon the infected subjects reached for their throats. Marisa checked the timer. Only thirty seconds and already the toxin was affecting their bloodstreams.

By the time she looked back at the chamber, blood was pouring from the noses and mouths of the infected monkeys. They lost control of their bladders and bowels then fell into their own excrement. One of the healthy monkeys was banging away at the partition that separated it from the others. The crazed pounding continued until the panel fell against the chamber's floor.

Marisa felt her blood rise. Professor Garrett would never trust her now. She'd been careless. She should have checked the partition. Marisa turned to the professor. "I'm sorry-"

"Shhh! Look!"

She followed his gaze. The excited monkey that had knocked down the dividing panel grabbed the dead monkeys, shook them. The agitated monkey's paws were smeared with blood and bodily waste. He sniffed his paws then leaned against the nearest wall. Marisa looked from the monkey to the professor and back again.

The monkey reached for its throat, began to bleed. It reached down and tried in vain to stop itself from urinating. The monkey's eyes rolled up in its head, and it fell over on its side into a pool of its own urine and blood.

Marisa stepped back and lowered her eyes. The professor stepped in front of her with a single bound.

She accepted her fate and met his gaze.

"Did you see what just happened?" he demanded.

"I...don't know what happened. I thought Marc had secured the partition..."

"No. The monkey! The last one to die was one of the healthy specimens."

Marisa still didn't understand. The two surviving subjects were huddled in their side of the chamber, as far away from the others as possible. She shrugged.

The professor grabbed her shoulders in his enthusiasm. "Don't you see? This test was more successful than we ever anticipated."

There was something she was missing, couldn't grasp. She felt Garrett shake her.

"If a healthy subject contacts an infected subject's bodily fluids after the introduction of the catalyst, while it is still active, the poison reacts with the healthy bloodstream and kills that subject."

Marisa realized what the professor was telling her. "The toxin is more lethal than we'd anticipated!" His fervor was contagious. "Do you think we'll get permission to do the final trial?"

The glint in his steely eyes answered her question before he spoke. "Oh yes. We will run this test on humans."

THE SACRIFICE

Brian leaned forward on the barstool and exhaled. He scanned the bar and tapped delicate fingers on his tin of exotic Camel cigarettes. He stopped tapping when he saw Robb coming out of the dance club. Brian smiled and started to stand, until he saw that Robb wasn't alone. He was with Peter. *Not Pete. Peter. Preppy bastard. Be the bigger man, even if you are shorter than him.* Brian stood and waved. "Robb. Peter."

Brian saw them stop, exchange a look, then continue toward him. Brian held up his drink. "You guys like a drink?"

Robb sat on the stool next to Brian's. "Sure. How've you been?"

Peter stood behind them and adjusted his Italian silk tie unnecessarily. "Is that just a Coke with a mixing straw, or did you finally get over Eddie and have Russ put some rum in there?"

Brian crushed his cigarette in the ashtray and stood. Had his knees not been trembling, he would have come up to Peter's shoulder. Peter, with his average build, easily had more weight and muscle than Brian. "What else did you tell him about me, Robb? About us?"

Robb rubbed his hands across his face and turned to Peter. He motioned with one finger across the throat for Peter to stop. Robb stood between them. "Brian, I didn't do it to hurt you." He grabbed Peter by the shoulder and turned him toward the door. "Don't be an ass. Let's just leave."

Brian watched Peter and Robb exit. He turned back to the bar and was about to call for his tab and grab his cigarette tin when he felt a cold draft from the door as it reopened. Thinking Robb might be coming back to talk to him, Brian looked to the doorway and saw a tall blond man enter the club.

The stranger sauntered up to the bar holding his black leather jacket in one hand. As he approached, Brian noticed the coal black shirt and how it draped over the well-toned chest and strapping arms. It must have been custom-made to fit that well. His black-wash Versace jeans housed an impressive bulge in the crotch. He was wearing black hiking boots, probably Timberlands. The blond man stood self-assured, radiating power, wealth, and sexual energy. The man's blue eyes coolly appraised Brian, and the man seemed to have made a decision in those few moments. "Would you like another drink?" he asked.

"Not right now, but would you care to join me?" Brian extended his hand in introduction. "I'm Brian." His hand was taken in a firm clasp.

"Karl."

Rusty, the bartender and sometimes bouncer, came over. "What would you like?"

Karl looked to Brian, who shook his head. "Armadale Vodka on the rocks. Lemon twist. Put it on Brian's tab. I'll close it out."

Rusty must have been hoping for a nice tip from the newcomer because he quickly brought the drink with not one, but three, slices of lemon. Karl looked at the total, added ten, slid the cash across the counter, and thanked Rusty.

The bartender smiled. "Let me know if you need anything else."

Brian and Karl talked for a while, and when it seemed an acceptable amount of time had passed, Brian agreed to go back to Karl's cabin. This November seemed colder than last, and Brian was freezing by the time they reached Karl's Wrangler. It was toasty inside the Jeep before they had gotten out of Harrisburg.

It was a long drive north, and Karl didn't say much. Brian began making small talk. Before he knew it, he was telling Karl about the time two years ago when he and Eddie had gotten into an argument because Brian wanted to have friends over for Thanksgiving dinner, but Eddie didn't. Eddie had left in a snit and went out drinking until early in the morning. On the way home, he lost control of the car he shouldn't have been driving and crashed into a tree. He lived long enough for Brian to see him one final time. Since then he'd tried to have some relationships, but nothing worked out. Maybe he wasn't ready for anything serious yet; he didn't know.

Brian didn't know what else to say, so they sat in silence for the rest of the journey. Karl finally pulled off the highway and picked up Rural Route 106. In the black of night, Brian couldn't tell how Karl found the path he eventually took that wound its way to the cabin.

Karl parked the Wrangler near the front door. Brian jumped out of the Jeep, and Karl led him inside. Brian sat on a comfortable leather couch. It was the color of butter cream and felt as smooth as butter cream around him. Karl started the fireplace and turned on some loud, thumping trance music. Brian stood up in anticipation and stripped Karl and himself. Karl forced Brian onto the couch.

Brian reclined and closed his eyes. Karl was quick and efficient. Brian looked down to watch and noticed that a tattoo was somewhat visible between Karl's shoulders. It might have been a monk holding a flag and riding a pale horse, but Brian was far too distracted to focus on the depiction. He'd ask Karl about it if...they...cuddled...after...ahhh!

Karl went out to the other room, and Brian heard him turn on the water. He was disappointed, but when Karl returned and stood in front of the couch, Brian leaned forward to eagerly return the favor. Karl ordered, "No. On the floor."

Brian knelt on the wooden floor. He was used to luxurious, plush carpet or a thick bedspread on a memory foam mattress. His knees were getting sore, and he hadn't even begun yet.

Karl grabbed Brian's head and roughly pulled Brian to him.

Brian felt it had taken forever. His knees were

sore and his legs stiff.

Karl went into the kitchen again and came back with some very bubbly champagne. He handed the glass to Brian. "Excuse me for a minute. I believe I left something in the Jeep."

When Karl stepped outside, Brian poured the alcoholic drink into the ice bowl. He was thirsty, but he'd made a promise on Eddie's deathbed, and he'd keep it.

Karl returned and saw the empty glass. His chiseled face broke into a smug grin, and he dressed. Brian reached over to pick up his own clothes, but Karl shoved him, and he pitched onto the floor. Karl's harsh words, "You die tonight," made Brian shiver although the fire still blazed.

Brian shook his head in confusion. He got back up onto his aching knees and tentatively reached for his pants. Karl kicked Brian solidly in the jaw with the rugged heel of his boot. Blood poured out of Brian's mouth. He rubbed his jaw and shook his head.

Karl taunted, "By the time I toss you into my Jeep, you'll be unconscious from the drug in your drink. Based on my experience, you'll come to when I start carving slices of your abominable flesh from your body. Fortunately for you, you're smaller than the others I've sacrificed. You'll probably only last a few hours." Karl laughed and went out to start the Wrangler.

Brian took advantage of the opportunity and grabbed a handful of his clothing. He ran to the kitchen and tried the back door. It was padlocked. He searched for another exit and noticed the large window over the kitchen sink. He climbed into the sink, balled the clothes around his fist, and smashed the window. He cleared the sharp edges with his clothes and climbed through the hole. *Damn it's cold up here.* Brian began to shake the glass from his garments when he heard Karl rush into the kitchen. He turned and saw Karl lifting a rifle or shotgun.

Brian ducked and flung his clothing through the window frame to obstruct Karl's aim. Blam! Brian scrambled away from the cabin on all fours. Too late he realized he was heading into the woods instead of toward the idling Jeep.

He hurried through the northern Pennsylvania forest. Wearing nothing on a cold, cloudy night in an unfamiliar place and with a rifle-toting murderer pursuing him, Brian was at a serious disadvantage. He stumbled forward, cutting his feet on rocks, and tripping over fallen tree limbs. He dropped to the ground when he saw the dirt road directly ahead.

Quickly peering into the darkness both up and down the road, Brian darted across the open area and into the trees and brush on the opposite side. He dived and rolled to a stop next to some tall trees. He listened for footsteps or the sound of an engine. Hearing nothing but the pounding of his heart and his own heavy breathing, he continued on. As Brian ran, his arms, chest, and legs were torn open by the jagged brush. Brian let out a stifled scream. He stopped, leaning forward, hands resting on his knees. He shook from exertion and tried to catch his breath, but the frigid air burned his lungs.

Brian was breathing so heavily and his teeth were chattering so hard that he barely heard the roar from the approaching Jeep's engine. When the sound registered, he dropped to the ground shivering. The spotlight mounted on the driver's side of the Jeep traced a path mere feet above Brian's prone body, but the vehicle continued on at breakneck speed, toward Rural Route 106.

Brian sobbed quietly as he stood. He rubbed his hands over his body, but it didn't help. He didn't know what to do. *The cabin? Can I find my way back? How could I defend it against Karl and his gun? My cell phone? Probably no signal. Middle of nowhere. Police would never find me in time. Keep moving. Highway. Another motorist. Only hope.*

Brian's feet were lacerated with open wounds. He swayed dizzily. In the dim light, he didn't see the tree root in front of him. Brian tripped over it, tumbled forward, and slid down a steep slope. As the rocks littering the frozen ground battered him, he screamed in agony. Brian's slide came to an abrupt halt when he rolled into the trunk of an aspen. He realized he could still feel pain at the same time he realized his ribs were broken.

He could only take in shallow gulps of air. The pain in his chest was too great when he tried to take a full breath. He struggled to stand and was about to give up when a twig snapped. Brian couldn't tell where the sound originated. In the still cold night, it could have been hundreds of yards away or only a few feet.

Adrenaline overrode the pain, and Brian stood, leaning against the tree. Brian looked around. There was no way he could get back up the rise even if he'd wanted to go in that direction. Everything else looked the same. He continued ahead, wheezing with every weak breath. He staggered forward, slumping against one tree, then another. Brian thought he saw movement to his right. He crumpled to the ground to hide.

He closed his eyes and panted. He didn't want to die like this, alone in the woods with a maniac. Through his closed eyes, he could tell it had gotten brighter. It was too intense to be the moon. Facing the inevitable, he slowly opened his eyes.

Karl looked down at him, flashlight in hand. Karl laughed as he unslung the rifle and aimed it at Brian's head.

Brian forced out one final word. "Why?"

The last thing he heard was the rifle blast. The force threw him to the ground. *Cold. Never knew death was so cold.*

DELIVERING THE GOODS

The khaki paintjob on the Deliveries Overnight Worldwide Now Service van looked new because it was just applied to a generic cargo van within the week. John Byrne brought the van to a smooth stop as he parked at the turnpike rest area. He locked it carefully, but to anyone who might be watching, he'd appear a carefree kid in his early twenties. If they were close enough and bothered to read what was stitched on the jumpsuit, they'd see he was Petey.

John Byrne had many names but preferred his middle name, Trevor. However, today his guise was Petey, a DOWNS parcel delivery boy. Because of his slouch, it was hard to tell he'd be six feet tall if you measured from his hiking boots to his dirty blond hair. Petey was an easy role to assume. The young guy who was too good-natured and trusting to realize everyone thought he was a nobody. Between his friendly demeanor and the recognizable khaki uniform, people ignored him. They didn't realize that today he would deliver death.

Petey ambled toward the brick and glass building and watched an old, beat-up Jeep Cherokee pull into an open space near the front of the plaza. Rust and gray primer showed through what remained of the original navy paint. The driver shouted at two shabbily dressed young boys who rushed out of the vehicle. Petey held the door for the boys and prepared to enter. The boys' father brushed past Petey, cutting him off. Petey sarcastically said, "You're welcome," but no one noticed.

Petey strolled inside and looked for the coffee stand. *Great.* The Jeep's driver stood at the end of the line for coffee and continued shouting at the children even though they were right in front of him. Petey stepped into line behind the man and pulled a $10 bill out of his pocket, so it would be ready when the cashier expected it. He knew from experience that this chain typically hired rude employees who didn't want to be bothered or kept waiting.

Trevor observed the man in line ahead of him. The loudmouth's wardrobe looked as old and worn as his Jeep. The tattered jeans were frayed at what remained of the cuffs and came down to the back of dirty sneakers. The man's casual shirt was buttoned. It hung loose, not tucked into the jeans. Between barking at the kids, the man ordered his coffee and cinnamon scone at full volume. Trevor was surprised. He would have pictured the loudmouth as a muffin man.

The girl at the counter took some time calculating the change. She finally handed it to her customer. He reached behind him to stuff the bills into a pocket, but they slid off his shirttail and fluttered to the floor. The man jerked the tray from the counter. "Took long enough," he said and ordered the boys to the burger stand for their breakfast.

Trevor bent down and retrieved the bills. Knowing no one would notice, he broke character long enough to fold them around the ten he was already holding. He rose and in his polite Petey voice tentatively called, "Excuse me. Mister."

The man turned sharply and in an even louder voice than normal boomed, "What?"

Petey held up the bills and courteously replied, "You dropped your money, sir."

The man pushed his tray toward the DOWNS boy. "Yeah, well, just throw it on here. And it better all be there." Petey placed the folded bills on the tray and turned to order his coffee. The man interrupted him. "Hey, kid."

Petey turned his head.

The man quietly said, "Thanks," then walked away to join his boys.

The smile on Petey's face was genuine. He turned back to the girl at the coffee stand, and she demanded, "Are you going to order?"

"Yeah, sure. I'll take a biggee morning blend." He waited until she turned to fill his order and then asked, "What was that other thing that guy just ordered?"

The cashier was in her early twenties, but rather than perky she seemed world-weary. She sighed heavily and rolled her eyes up before answering. "It was a cinnamon scone." She filled the coffee cup and placed it on the counter.

"I think I'll try one of those cinnamon cones, too,"

Petey said, purposely mispronouncing the word and nodding his head in confirmation. "That looked kind of good." The girl shook her head and silently got the scone. She rang up the order and waited for Petey to dig small bills out of his pocket to pay. He thanked her and went over to the stand with the sugar and creamer. Petey poured some half and half into his coffee and spilled some on the counter when he pulled the carafe away from his cup. "Ooops." He snapped a plastic lid onto his cup and grabbed a napkin to mop up the spill. He wiped off the counter, grabbed a few more napkins, and found a vacant seat.

He took a small sip and confirmed that it was nowhere near as good as the Gevalia Peruvian or Jamaican coffee Trevor would have made at home. Oh well, he was used to tough conditions in the field.

Trevor's cursory scan of the lounge area provided the usual glimpse of families and business people sitting uncomfortably on cheap but sturdy chairs. He was pleased to see that the man and his two boys were quietly shoveling their breakfasts into their mouths.

The smell of hot coffee and frozen breakfast pastries, which had been partially, but not thoroughly, reheated completed the bland ambiance.

He saw nothing suspicious, so he enjoyed his scone, and his view of the busty redhead two tables away, who sat staring at her unopened pack of Marlboro Menthol Lights. Red sat alone. Staring. She was in less of a hurry than the other patrons. As she drank a slow sip of coffee, he noticed she was wearing several rings, but none on the finger that mattered. Had she left someone behind? Was she going somewhere new or just going? Whichever it was, Red seemed to be reassessing her decision.

Trevor hated uncertainty in his own life. He was typically decisive and sure of himself, but he continued to question the decision to end his engagement to Cindy. He couldn't forget her, at least not yet. Ever? Life was full of decisions, and he had to live with the ones he made. Regret wouldn't kill him as quickly as a bullet. No, it would spread slowly like cancer and his life might just as well be over. *Enough of that.*

He pushed his thoughts of Cindy aside, drank more coffee and looked again at the pensive redhead. Red's light gray eyes and fiery mane emphasized her pale skin. Trevor didn't remember why, but he associated gray eyes with cold women. If he had been returning from his assignment, he would have tried to strike up a conversation anyway to see where it led. Since he was on his way to eliminate a problem, however, there wasn't time for Red this morning.

Petey swallowed the rest of the coffee. On his way to the restroom, he walked to Red's table. He stopped, gave a goofy smile, and said, "Hi." Red glanced up. When she saw his khaki uniform, she sneered and went back to studying her still unopened box of cigarettes. Petey continued, undaunted. "I can't believe you haven't opened those yet. Do you want to go outside and have a smoke? I could use a menthol light right now. That cool minty tobacco taste is the best."

She glared at him and finally spoke. "Buy your own and leave me the hell alone." Her harsh voice was even colder than her gray eyes.

Petey made and broke eye contact several times as he replied, "You don't know how hard it is for a guy to approach a woman. If you're not interested, 'no thanks' is fine. There's no need to swear at me." He trudged off, his shoulders slumped.

Trevor continued on to the restroom confident his disguise was effective.

When he washed up at the sink, he examined his reflection in the cracked mirror. With the baggy uniform, youthful hairstyle, and his raven hair dyed blond, Trevor looked more like a lanky kid in his early twenties than the well-toned thirty eight year old government agent he had become. It was all a matter of perception. He felt good but didn't have the same energy and stamina he did fifteen years ago. Perhaps those years of experience made up for what age had taken away? Trevor's naturally brown eyes looked back at him, reflecting his easygoing smile. With a youthful gait, he returned to the parking lot.

Although it was a typical DOWNS van, the contents it carried were far from the usual business and personal freight. Trevor knew from the surveys and recon photos he'd studied that he wouldn't have enough practical cover to get within range of his target with the Heckler & Koch MSG90 sniper rifle that was nestled snugly in a specially marked shipping carton in the back. No, if he were going to succeed, he would once again rely primarily on his dual SW99 .45s. The baggy jacket hid both the pistol in his shoulder holster as well as the one inside the waistband at the small of his back.

Some of his colleagues thought he was overly cautious with his preparations and training, but he was alive. Several field agents he had known weren't. He considered himself pragmatic. Each mission could be his last. Trevor credited exercise, martial arts, and frequent combat and weapons practice with his survival to date. Without these, he certainly wouldn't have returned from his last assignment in west Los Angeles.

Trevor had made good time since he'd started the trip in the darkness of early morning. Now, there were more cars and campers on the road, but traffic was far from heavy. As he approached New York, he enjoyed the beauty of the colorful golden and red leaves that still had not fallen. Soon they too would fall, and the barren trees would look even more lifeless than the clerk who had waited on Petey at the coffee stand.

A few minutes after eleven, Trevor pulled up to the gate of a mansion far removed from the nearest New York suburb. The place was apparently as much a fortress as a luxury home. The bulky guard in the bulletproof gatehouse called out over the speaker, "You need something?"

Trevor smiled to the guard and looked at his electronic data pad. "Yes, sir. I have a package for P.

Eneas Cowen. I'll need his signature to release it. Is he here?"

"I'll sign. What is it?"

Petey smiled and leaned forward to make a point of examining the estate. "Man, this place is huge. I don't know what's in it, but the package is heavy. Do you want me to leave it here, or should I go on up to the house, mister?"

The guard stepped out of the gatehouse and squinted into the midday sun. "Just show me where to sign and leave the damn thing here, kid."

Petey held out the data pad but let go just before the man had a chance to grasp it. Without thinking, the guard bent down and retrieved it. As he looked up to ask for the stylus, he saw the .45 pointed directly at his head. "Open the gate then get in the driver's seat. And no alarms or you're a dead man." There was now steel in the voice and the left-hand grip, which kept the semi-automatic leveled on the guard, was easy but unwavering. Petey stepped out of the truck. The formerly friendly brown eyes had turned icy and convinced the guard that now was not the time for heroics.

Lacking the opportunity to attempt closing the gatehouse door behind him, the guard hit a button, and the gate slid open. After Petey backed into the van, the guard climbed into the driver's seat. Petey ordered, "With your right hand, slowly throw your gun off to the side of the gate." The guard hesitated for a split second as he considered swinging his weapon around, but he wisely tossed it away before driving to the mansion.

Resembling a scaled down version of an ancient cathedral door, the heavy steel reinforced barrier opened soundlessly moments after the doorbell was rung. The man who answered was even stockier than the first guard. "Jim, what the hell are you doing here? You should be at the gate."

"Hey, Leo. I know it's a little unusual and all, but this DOWNS boy has a delivery for Mr. Cowen."

Keeping the .45 aimed at Jim's back, Petey stepped forward. "Sorry to bother you guys, but I can't release the merchandise until I get positive acceptance. Could you please ask Mr. Cowen to come here for just a minute?"

Although Trevor couldn't see Jim's face, he could tell Jim was sending Leo a message. Leo dropped and rolled behind the wall. Trevor blew the expression off Jim's face from behind with one hollowpoint round. He shoved the corpse through the doorway. Leo fired several shots, and Jim's body jerked unnaturally before it fell to the floor.

For the last six years, Trevor unfailingly loaded his gun alternating hollowpoints followed by armor-piercing rounds. However, being unable to see where Leo was hiding, there was no sure way to shoot him without entering the home or luring him outside.

Fortunately, like Petey, the data pad was more than it appeared. Ducking below the window and crawling forward, Trevor stopped within arm's reach of the entrance. He set the data pad to his side and kept his eyes riveted to the open doorway. Without looking, he pressed the buttons in a practiced sequence and immediately hurled the data pad into the room. He silently counted to himself. When he reached five, he threw his arm in front of his face and closed his eyes. The flash grenade's brilliance quickly dissipated, and Trevor spun through the opening using the door's frame as partial cover. Leo was trying to get his bearings. Instead, he got three bullets in the chest. The rounds exited the gaping hole in his back, and blood spurted across the shell white wall in a pattern the painter had never foreseen.

Trevor had used four rounds, leaving six in the gun he was holding and another ten in the one under his shoulder. He also carried three back-up clips with nine rounds each. The recon reports indicated Cowen had as many as five bodyguards total, typically on staggered shifts. There should also be a maid and butler somewhere in the mansion at this time of day. Both Kandi and her husband were confirmed present prior to Trevor's arrival. He had gained access and already eliminated over twenty percent of the estimated opposition.

Once inside, Trevor saw little, if any, trustworthy cover. Trevor knew that the other guards on duty would have heard the racket and would come running. He briefly considered pushing forward until he saw the barrels of two full automatics rounding either side of the adjoining hallway. Without waiting to glimpse what the gunmen looked like, Trevor dived out the front door. He rushed to the railing, vaulted over it with one hand, and sprinted to his van. Trevor broke a cold sweat when he heard the thud of bullets pounding the doorway, railing, dirt, and his van.

Trevor would be an easy mark if he stopped now to break out some heavier artillery, so he gunned the idling engine and drove to one side of the vast house. It would be much easier to avoid being surrounded from here—as long as nobody got to the upstairs balcony before he did. Throwing off the jacket, he unlocked the inside door to the back of the truck and quickly strapped a bandoleer of grenades across his chest. He grabbed the parcel containing the Uzi submachine gun and glanced out the driver's side door. The two guards were not yet in sight. Trevor lobbed a grenade at the corner of the house he expected them to come from and waited inside the van for the explosion before he carefully climbed to the van's roof. No one was on the balcony, so he tossed the box onto the ledge, ran across the roof of the vehicle, and jumped.

He just missed grabbing the rail and, instead, barely caught one of the posts with his right hand. His weight pulled him down, and he almost lost his grip on the post when his fist slammed into the floor of the balcony. Trevor swung his legs and caught the edge of the overhang with his left hand. He pulled himself up and then dropped over the railing onto his back. The door behind him slid open. Trevor whipped the gun out of his shoulder holster and aimed it at the unarmed man's chest. The butler spoke. "Mr. Cowen will see you now."

Trevor stood and nodded. "Thank you." The butler was an athletic man in his early fifties. Keeping the gun trained on the butler's back, the agent followed him inside to the luxurious guestroom. The furnishings and artwork were impressive and very expensive. Trevor didn't attempt to guess the artist or designer. That wasn't his field of expertise. Instead, he looked around considering cover he could use if needed and where an enemy might hide. The room looked safe enough for the moment.

The butler neared the room's exit and turned to face the uninvited guest. He gestured to Trevor's left and told him, "This way, sir." The butler stepped out of the room and crooked his head faintly to the right before turning smartly to the left.

Trevor realized someone was standing outside the doorway. If they still wanted to kill him and waited until he was in the corridor, he might not have time to react. *Hope it's not Cowen. No, he wouldn't have the balls to do it himself.* Trevor fired rounds into the wall just right of the doorway and ran backwards to the sliding door. He stopped firing when his gun locked open. The hollowpoints may have been stopped by studs, but at least the alternating rounds made contact with lethal force. The would-be assailant cried out in surprise before falling across the doorway.

Trevor thumbed the magazine release. The empty clip dropped from his SW99. He slammed one of the three spares into the pistol with enough force to bring the slide forward and chamber the top round. He holstered the pistol and then ripped open the box he'd thrown onto the balcony. Trevor pulled out the Uzi.

Trevor crouched and returned to the empty guestroom. Three guards down. At most that should leave another two, the butler, maid, the subject, and his wife. Some experts advised gamblers to take their winnings and go to a different casino before the odds caught up to them. Trevor didn't have that option. He had to keep pressing his luck against this house.

He peered into the hallway in both directions and saw no threat. Assuming the butler had tried to mislead him completely, Trevor warily made his way to the room at the right end of the corridor. Pushing the door open, he scanned the room with the Uzi ready.

The master suite was even more majestic than the guestroom. The word sprawling came to Trevor's mind. The craftsmanship of the dresser, chairs, sofa, and other assorted furnishings was impressive. A king-sized bed with a custom cabinet frame made of the same exotic wood as the other furniture was the centerpiece of the room, or it would have been, if Kandi Cowen had not been standing in front of the full-length mirror wearing only a black silk bra and matching see-through panties.

Trevor knew from his briefing that Kandi was much younger than her wealthy husband, and she looked decent in the photos he'd studied. Obviously, she didn't photograph well because she was stunning in the flesh. Her blonde hair was done in a short, professional style; her well-rounded breasts in a large, professional style. Whatever she did to keep tanned and trim certainly worked.

Kandi turned around to face him, her azure eyes wide at the sight of the unknown man and his weapons. When she moved, he could smell her perfume. He didn't know what brand it was, but the floral scent was intoxicating—or maybe it was her beauty. "Please don't kill me. I'm worth a ton of money alive." She cast her eyes downward as if to ensure he took in her body and then looked back up into his eyes. Her deep blue eyes seemed to be pleading.

Trevor felt the stirrings in his loins and was again grateful that his loose fitting clothes were good for concealment. Trying to keep his voice firm, he asked, "Where is your husband?"

Kandi stepped closer and pulled her bra off over her head. Her full yet firm breasts jutted out, and the flushed nipples pointed at him. "Who cares?"

Trevor knew this was crazy, but it had been a while since he'd been with a woman, especially one this fine. Trevor smiled and breathed faster, pleasantly drowning in the floral perfume. It was important to stop and smell the roses, especially one this fragrant. Rose—that was the flowery fragrance engulfing him.

Kandi was close enough to hold when Trevor noticed motion in the mirror behind her—an armed man had sneaked up the hallway behind him. Trevor grabbed Kandi's upper arm and shoved her to safety then pivoted and let loose with the Uzi. The surprised guard was practically cut in two along the line of his solar plexus. His final reflex was to fire one shot that went wild before he dropped his gun and toppled backwards to the now blood-soaked carpet.

Kandi stood and nodded her head toward the bed in invitation. Trevor asked, "How close are you and your husband?"

Kandi walked to the nightstand and lit a cigarette. She held in the smoke for a moment before answering. "That old has been? You'd think he'd always want to be with me, but we never spend time together anymore. And since the trial, he can't even...satisfy me." She took another drag on the cigarette and continued, "If you kill him, make sure they can identify the body. I don't want any trouble with the life insurance people." She wrote down the number to her cell phone. "When this blows over, call me."

Trevor had survived this long by being both cautious and frosty. Okay, and sometimes lucky. Even with everything going on around him, he felt something growing for the blonde. He wanted to touch her, taste her. He only took the note. He set his jaw, and his deep brown eyes once again became windows to his frigid heart.

Eneas looked upstairs when he heard gunfire erupt again. He paced. He continued to pace. Still Troy didn't return with a status report. Eneas assumed the worst. He didn't care what happened to the cheap whore of a wife he'd married when he was a rising executive, but good help like Troy was damned hard to find. Troy was loyal and faithful unlike Eneas' slut wife. Troy was sneaky like her though. Son of a bitch could come up right behind someone, and he wouldn't have a damn clue until it was too late.

"Elwood!" he snapped. "Fetch my Hummer. Now!"

"Very well, sir," the butler replied and hurried to carry out his master's wishes.

Eneas looked around and saw his maid shrinking in the kitchen. "This house is a damn mess. I want it immaculate when I return." At least she still trembled in fear of him. Things were beginning to slip through his grasp here, and he didn't like it. He walked out.

Trevor worked his way downstairs without seeing anyone else until he reached the kitchen. The maid shook as she took off her apron and walked toward the door. From the dark hair and her skin tone, Trevor thought she might be Hispanic. Trevor asked, "Where's your boss?"

When she turned around, he realized she was Asian, possibly Vietnamese. He also realized from the deep red coloring of her face that she was flushed with anger. "Him tell me to clean house and him leave. Screw him!" She stuck up her middle finger towards the door. "Me no clean this mess. I quit."

Trevor watched her storm through the doorway.

He followed her outside. Trevor saw a vehicle speeding down the road and knew it had to be Cowen. Trevor would never catch up in the DOWNS van. He rushed past the maid to the garage behind the house and gave the remaining car collection a quick once over. The luxury cars were obviously armor plated security vehicles, but the Porsche Boxster S was pure sports car. He found the Porsche key ring on the wall, grabbed it off the hook, and jumped over the driver's door. The throaty growl of the exhaust told Trevor he would catch his quarry.

The icy rush of wind whipped through the convertible and chilled Trevor. He was intent on catching Cowen before the criminal reached civilization. He didn't have time to take his eyes off the road and look for the control to close the cockpit. Besides, even though it might make him an easier target if Cowen or the driver had a gun, keeping the top down would give Trevor a larger potential field of fire.

He wound out the gears to get as much speed as possible from the machine. There was only one street in and out of this isolated area. Trevor soon spotted the vehicle ahead. Seconds later, he determined it was a modified Hummer H2. The heavy SUV had a powerful engine, but the Hummer would never outrun the German sports car and its precision engineering. Trevor pulled alongside the Hummer and motioned for the driver to stop on the berm of the road. Instead, the butler swerved toward the Porsche.

Trevor instinctively adjusted his car's position on

the road while removing a grenade from the bandoleer around his chest. He needed to finish this soon. If anyone saw him wearing the grenades and called the police, his mission would be over in a hurry. He raced ahead of the Hummer and pulled the pin to make the grenade live. He dropped the grenade out of the car and continued ahead. The grenade exploded as the Hummer reached it, shredding the left front tire. The Hummer jerked and slowed.

Trevor downshifted and made a U-turn. The Hummer was heading straight toward the Porsche. He reached under his arm and pulled out the SW99. The fresh clip he'd inserted in the guestroom had an armor-piercing round on top. That round was now chambered. He prolonged the game of chicken until the last possible moment before he moved into the other lane. Trevor aimed as well as he could while keeping his Porsche safely on the road. He fired a single shot. The safety glass next to the butler exploded. The butler slammed on the brake when the bullet entered his temple. It was the last conscious act he made.

Trevor turned the Porsche around and parked behind the Hummer. Cowen stormed out. "What the hell do you want?"

"Money. How much is your life worth to you?" Trevor asked.

"How much do you think I have left?"

Because of the special deal Trevor had negotiated when accepting this assignment, he would get a tax-free cut of twenty-five percent of any money recovered from this criminal. "Well, the papers say you embezzled about sixty million dollars from your company. Even with your extravagant lifestyle, I'd say you are still sitting on about...thirty million."

Eneas spit. "Like hell. It's spent. Do you have any idea what my attorney fees cost? And you can't even begin to imagine how fast my hussy wife can go through cash. All of it is gone, gone, gone."

Trevor raised his pistol and pointed it directly at Eneas' heart—or where one would be if he actually had one in there. "Then there's nothing more to discuss. Except for meeting your wife, this was a waste of my time."

"Wait! I have a Swiss bank account. I completely forgot. I could wire you the money in that account. Just over five hundred thousand."

"I'm going to give you one last chance. Can you think of a way to come up with fifteen million before I count to three? One...two..."

"Five million. I can get you five. Follow me back to my house. We'll make the transfer there," the businessman said in a final attempt at controlling the situation.

Trevor reached for a grenade and stopped. Eneas flinched. The embezzler had been dominant and fearless in the boardroom but was now out of his element. Trevor saw the fear in the businessman's eyes. Instead of the explosive, Trevor grabbed his cell phone and held it out for Eneas to take. "Make the call right here. I'll give you the information you'll need to make the transfer. After I confirm it's available, I'm gone."

Eneas snatched the phone out of Trevor's hand. Eneas snapped the top up and pushed the numbers. He hesitated and looked at Trevor. The agent gestured with the gun for Eneas to continue. Eneas stabbed the send button. He authorized the transfer of five million dollars from his Swiss account to one Trevor's agency had established under a fictitious name at another Swiss bank.

"You made that look real easy. You wouldn't be holding out on me, would you?"

Eneas glowered at the agent and shook his head. He closed the phone and tossed it away. Trevor didn't fall for the mundane distraction. The agent kept the gun trained on Eneas until the businessman's shoulders slumped. If looks could kill, Trevor would be pushing up daisies.

"Get down on all fours. Now! Crawl over and get my phone. If you stand, you die." Trevor listened to the man curse as he went to retrieve the cell phone.

Eneas picked up the phone and looked confused. "Can I walk it back to you?"

"Slip it in your shirt pocket and crawl back."

The man continued cursing and finally returned. He held the phone out, and Trevor took it.

The agent considered harassing the former executive further but didn't want to divert the man from a possible last minute change of heart. "You can stand, but don't make any sudden moves. Don't you feel a little better now? Like maybe you want to ask

God to forgive you and turn over a new leaf?" Allowing Eneas time to repent, as well as for the bank to transfer the funds, Trevor waited. *Give me a reason to let you live.* Trevor hoped he'd glimpse some potential for good from Eneas before Trevor confirmed the wire transfer.

Instead, Eneas paced back and forth alongside his utility vehicle and spent the time cursing and muttering about making the "son of a bitch pay" for this someday. Minutes later, Trevor called and ascertained that the funds had been deposited.

Disappointed that the brash businessman had just squandered the few remaining minutes of his life, the agent looked into Eneas' eyes and demanded, "How could you steal from the trusting and dedicated people who worked for you? You embezzled their life savings. They lost everything they worked hard for and set aside for retirement. And, on top of that, they lost their jobs. How many families did you destroy?"

Eneas stopped pacing near the end of the truck. He turned to face the agent and laughed heartily. "You said it earlier, kid, it was only about money. The opportunity was there. Like any good capitalist, I capitalized on it. I seized it with both hands. That's how people get rich in this country, kid."

The comment hit Trevor close to home, but he had earned his fortune delivering justice for the United States government. The people he destroyed deserved it. He shrugged off the remark, opened the Porsche's trunk and placed the bandoleer inside. He considered the grenades momentarily but remembered Kandi's request and closed the trunk. *Maybe a grenade down the throat would be more brutal than even this bastard deserved. Probably not, but that's beside the point.*

Trevor drew the SW99 from the small of his back. He pointed the muzzle at the road between him and the corporate raider and contemplated the deadly weapon. At this range, he wouldn't want to chance hitting the H2's gas tank with an armor-piercing round. He thought back. *One round on Jim and another three on Leo. Four rounds. A hollowpoint would be in the chamber.*

Eneas' laughter abruptly ended. "What the hell are you doing, boy? I paid you off. I bought you, fucker!" He backed up against the Hummer, eyes searching hopelessly for a passing motorist. Trevor was grateful Cowen had purchased a secluded manor in New York instead of a property in the heart of Beverly Hills or a similarly busy locale.

Trevor raised the gun. "I was never for sale, dick." He squeezed the trigger. Eneas slid down the fender, leaving a trail of blood that began to pool as he slumped against the large tire.

Short of a paramedic helicopter choosing this spot for an unscheduled landing, Kandi would become a wealthy widow. Trevor confirmed that he still had her number. They had unfinished business, but it must wait. For now, he'd satisfied both his primary and secondary mission goals: objective elimination and monetary recovery.

Trevor raised the Porsche's top and confiscated

an expensive ballpoint from its glovebox. He turned over the paper with Kandi's phone number and wrote the vehicle's identification number on the opposite side. Then, Trevor kept his word and was gone.

THE USUAL SUBJECTS

Ray Peters heard the main door to the stucco apartment building close behind the newspaper delivery man. Ray quietly opened the door to his unit and looked around. No one else was in the hallway yet. He might not have much time. He had to act now. He sprinted down the hallway and snatched the plastic bag containing his neighbor's copy of this morning's *Patriot-News*. He ran back and quickly closed his door.

He poured water into his coffee maker and hoped the leftover grounds would still have enough flavor to brew one more cup. He shot a glance at the stack of unpaid bills piled on his table. Swatara Township, Pennsylvania wasn't the most expensive place to live, but he really needed to find a way to score some quick cash. If he couldn't find something promising in the classified section today, he was going to have to find a woman and crash at her place.

He poured the weak coffee into a dirty mug. He picked up a plastic container, but there was no powdered creamer left. He threw the empty container toward the trash can and cursed as it bounced off the rim and rolled across the floor. He sat on an old chair at a battered kitchen table and found the section of the newspaper he was looking for.

He couldn't believe his luck when he saw an ad titled "EASY MONEY." He read it twice and reached for the phone. He held his breath and hit the talk button. He smiled when he heard the dial tone. Things were looking up!

"She's old enough to find a damn job and support herself. Or let her rent some section eight slum and collect welfare. I didn't work hard all these years to come home at night and not have any damn privacy, woman."

Monikwa Baker tried to calm her husband, Leroy. This anger couldn't be good for his blood pressure. "She just needs more time. She'll find something soon."

"It's been two damn years already! We raised our girl. Must not have done too good from the looks of things, but I put in my time. Either they're out come the new year, or I'm out. Period." Satisfied with his tie's knot, he entered the closet and chose a matching sport coat.

She walked up behind him, rested her head on his shoulder, and wrapped her arms around his stomach. It had grown considerably over the last two years, and there was no doubt why. "What about her illness? How can you just throw her out?"

Without saying another word, Leroy removed his wife's arms and left for his office. Mrs. Baker wept silently as she finished dressing. After she wiped away her tears, she put on her makeup and smiled.

The smile was forced, but at least the lipstick wasn't smeared, and the mascara hadn't run.

Hoping Deanne and Justin didn't hear today's fight, she went downstairs to get a cup of coffee and an English muffin smothered with butter substitute.

Her daughter was already awake and pouring over the classified ads yet again. "Morning, honey. Find anything today?" she asked.

Deanne looked up. "Not yet. The only places willing to talk to a dropout, single mother are the golden arches and the superstore that sells all that stuff made in China. Shit, those places ain't even worth my time, 'specially since I'd need to take the bus or get a ride."

"Deanne, your daddy wants you and Justin out by the end of the year. You need to find a way to support yourself."

Deanne stood and shouted, "Momma, I been trying since I moved back! How do I get a job in a few weeks when I ain't got one yet?"

"How hard you been trying? Maybe you should just find a man to live with. What about that nice white boy, Marc? He has a good job. He could take care of you two. And he lives right here in Steelton."

"Marc got fired for embezzlement! Last I heard, he was selling used cars at one of the dealers over on Paxton Street. Besides, he was too short and his breath was always nasty."

"So he's not in jail?"

"I don't think so."

"Well then, I'm sure he's making enough to

support the three of you. Until you find a job of your own. Why not call him?"

"Momma!"

"Is that boy of yours ready for school, or is he taking the bus?"

Deanne went to the stairway and yelled, "Justin, get down here and go with Nanny!"

Justin lumbered down the stairs with his head down. He was overweight from too many snack cakes. His pullover sweater barely covered his gut, and the collar of the white shirt was smeared with chocolate. "Hi, Nanny. Bye, Mom." Deanne hugged her son, careful to avoid the chocolate stain.

Mrs. Baker took Justin, leaving Deanne alone.

Deanne was finally alone again. She enjoyed being alone, especially in the early morning. Peace and quiet. *No husband to slap me around and demand kinky sex. Call Marc! Hell, that boy was a freak too. Always going on about having an Asian join them. When I finally agreed and found that skinny jailbait teenager to do it for fifty bucks, that little shit Marc kept saying, "Oh, Kay," and spent most of the time with the Asian bitch. Damn ho didn't even have any junk in the trunk!*

Deanne drank her instant coffee and focused on the classified ads. She needed money, and she needed it soon. Dropping out of high school to raise Justin had been a huge mistake. After all those years of beating on her and cheating on her, DJ had passed on a number of sexually transmitted diseases and then left her for a high school senior because he wanted an educated woman!

Her parents refused to watch Justin. Deanne was stuck being responsible for her childhood mistake. Thank God for the boy's school. It gave her a chance to relax and watch her favorite game shows and soaps. She especially enjoyed watching *What's My Price?* and *The Young and Breastless*.

She was about to stop her daily ritual of glancing at notices and flipping pages when an ad under "EASY MONEY" caught her attention.

Leading gene research corporation seeks subjects for experimental testing of new treatment we anticipate will wipe out HIV and AIDS forever. Applicants must authorize release of medical records prior to testing. To apply call 1-866-GENETIC. Successful candidates will be well compensated. Call today. Testing begins Friday.

Terrific! Not only could she earn money, but maybe even get free treatment for her AIDS. God only knew what they'd charge once they were allowed to sell the shit. Deanne grabbed the phone off the wall and figured out what numbers to dial.

The call was answered quickly. A computerized voice prompted her through a series of questions. Deanne thought she would need to push numbers on the phone to answer but was amazed that the system could understand her spoken replies. If any company in the world could eliminate AIDS, it would be one with cutting-edge technology like this! Her excitement grew during the long interview.

After completing the series of questions the computer announced, "Your application has been approved. Please hold. You will be connected to a testing specialist in the order your call was received."

"Good morning, Miss Baker. I'm Technician Redman. Are you available to come to our lab Friday morning and stay through sometime Monday?"

She had expected to be on hold forever, so she was surprised when her call was picked up so soon. Surely her parents would watch the kid over the holiday weekend for an opportunity like this. "Oh yes, of course, I am!"

"Terrific, Miss Baker. Our lab is located on Kreider Drive in Middletown. Do you know how to get here?"

"I'll probably have to take a cab. I'm sure the driver will be able to find it."

"Kreider is off Oberlin Road near Fulling Mill Road and 283. When he turns off Oberlin and onto Kreider, you'll soon see our lab on your left. Be sure to arrive before ten a.m. Did you get all of that?"

Deanne repeated the details back to him. She gave the technician her parents' phone number, thanked him twice, and hung up the phone.

She felt so good about how this morning started that she began to tingle. She looked at the wall clock. Twenty minutes before *What's My Price?* started. Just enough time. Deanne smiled and hurried to her bedroom. Opening the panty drawer, she found the object she suddenly desired. She dialed the knob at the bottom to test the batteries. It hummed and vibrated in her hands, and she fell onto her bed. *Oh, that was good.* Deanne floated in a calm she had not felt for the last several years.

Breathing more rapidly, she turned the dial to full speed and shuddered in climax. She felt incredibly relaxed and decided some things in life were more important than TV programs. This would be a great day for a Baker's dozen.

Morgan Jenkins knelt on the floor next to his bed as he finished his morning prayers. He stood and placed his *Book of Mormon* on his nightstand then carefully set his leather-bound *New International Version Student Bible* on top of it.

He removed his plush navy robe from the closet and wore it over his striped flannel pajamas. Now warm, Morgan walked through the living room of his apartment and retrieved *The Patriot-News*. He'd heard that Mr. Lincoln downstairs hadn't been receiving his morning paper lately, but Morgan hadn't had any problems with his delivery.

Morgan rose early enough to do his daily devotional reading and still have time to make himself a hearty breakfast before he faced the hectic world of food service. Four slices of French toast, four sausage links, and a large glass of orange juice would get him through the day.

He scanned through the classified ads as he ate. Although he usually earned enough from tips to pay the bills, the diner didn't figure prominently in his long range employment plans.

Morgan finished his breakfast and turned to the last page of job opportunities. One ad caught his attention, but it wasn't for employment. He read the ad quickly. He could use the money but felt it would be the Christian thing to make one phone call first. He briefly wondered if the number would ring through or if he'd get a message advising him that the line had been disconnected.

"Yeah?"

"Ray, it's Morgan."

"Mo. What's up?"

"I was looking at the paper today and saw an ad. I thought you might be interested."

"Thanks, but I have some good leads already. I don't..."

"Ray, this isn't for a job. It's to earn money letting some lab run some tests on you."

There was a long pause. Morgan thought maybe the phone company had just shut off Ray's line. "Oh that? Yeah, I'm already signed up. Hey! You should see if they'd want you, too!"

"I'll do that." Morgan hung up the phone and muttered, "Thanks for telling me about it." He picked up the ad and punched in the toll-free number.

COINCIDENCE?

On the drive south, Trevor called Earl Waters, his case manager, to report. Within minutes, wheels would be set in motion that would recover the DOWNS van and steer the investigation of Mr. Cowen's untimely death away from Trevor.

"Our buddy Eneas wanted to transfer the title for his Porsche over to me. Only has 1,868 miles. You have your pen and notepad ready for the VIN?"

"What makes you think I'm not logged in to Maryland's DMV and completing the authorization as we speak?"

"Come on, Earl. We both know how much you trust computers." Trevor laughed and read off the Porsche's VIN. The Maryland department of motor vehicles would receive the required paperwork to confirm the sale and authorize transfer of the title into Trevor's name. He carefully put the paper back into his pocket to ensure he wouldn't lose Kandi's phone number, which was written on the other side.

Trevor returned to Maryland in time to attend his Monday evening martial arts classes. The Japanese dojo taught aikido, jo, and even kenjutsu. He'd trained in these martial forms for a few years and had a rudimentary knowledge of all three; however, each of these arts could take a lifetime of study to master.

The unarmed aikido class seemed the most practical of the three. Using the opponent's attack against him was a skill the agent had often put to use in his career. Aikido complemented the periodic hand-to-hand combat training he received from his employer.

The stick and sword training might not prove extremely relevant in a modern combat situation, but Trevor had been fond of handheld weapons since he was a child. *What would my parents think if they were still alive to know the cap guns and BB guns they bought me when I was young were forerunners to the everyday equipment I carry for my chosen profession?*

Before entering the dojo, Trevor removed the shirt that identified him as Petey and threw it on the floor of the car. The plain t-shirt and khaki pants wouldn't attract attention, but the DOWNS top bearing someone else's name might have been questioned. He walked inside, opened his locker, and changed into his martial arts uniform.

Trevor removed the silk bag, which protected his katana and saya. A Japanese swordsmith had customized the weapon from an ancient battle blade. The blade's original owner was an honorable samurai, who had protected his lord and the lord's lands. His lord had departed this life due to some natural cause. After the funeral ceremony, rather than become a ronin, the samurai had given up the way of the sword and become a monk. The sword was found hidden in the monk's chamber after he, too, had died.

The reconstructed sword had cost Trevor several thousand dollars and was the most expensive weapon he owned.

Trevor went to the mat, respectfully performed the ritual bow, and practiced drawing the sword and making various cuts. When the blade whistled through the air, Trevor knew his form was true. Unfortunately, he could only make the sword whistle about half the time. He had already worked up a sweat by the time the jo class began.

When Trevor turned onto his street, he saw cars parked along both sides, almost to the corners. He wasn't surprised to see which driveway was full. The Ferrells were having another house party.

He drove up the driveway of a large two-story, the fourth house on the right. The other homes on the block were all red brick with various colors of vinyl siding. Trevor preferred the look of stone and had ordered it for the entire home, not just the front or first level. A walk-up landing led to the front door. The enclosed rear deck with the sunken hot tub gave Trevor a private place to sit outside and relax with a drink and a cigar. It was an ideal solution, and he used it frequently.

Trevor eased the Porsche into the unused bay of his attached two-car garage. He pressed the button on the wall and closed the garage door. Before the light timed off, he entered his home.

Trevor went to his desk to check his mail. Nothing important. His bills were stacked with the ones due soonest on top. The envelopes had been stamped and the bills inserted. The completed checks were tucked under the envelope flaps and only needed to be signed. The junk mail had already been shredded. His part-time housekeeper, Anna, was not only attractive but also reliable and efficient. Finding her had been a stroke of luck.

He picked up his copy of *The Week* newsmagazine and noticed the Jos. A. Banks catalog that had been under it. Anna had marked a suit she liked in the catalog. He could use a new suit or two, and Anna's taste in men's clothing had been complimented by more than one woman he'd met.

Trevor scrubbed his hands at the sink and went to his bar. He dropped three ice cubes into a heavy crystal glass, poured in a generous shot of 12-year old Chivas Regal and nearly topped off the glass with Canada Dry Ginger Ale. He grabbed a key lime from the fridge, rinsed it under hot water, and cut the small lime in half. He squeezed in the juice from one half and left the other piece on the counter, knowing he'd soon be back for a refill. He took a long swallow and savored the blended scotch as it warmed him.

Trevor was the only human who lived in the house now that Cindy was gone, but another female still had her own room within. He opened the first of the doors to what he termed the "airlock" and closed it behind him. He was in a short passageway between two doors. The airlock was designed so the animal behind the next door would not have free run of the house if she got past the inside door before it could be closed. When he opened the second door, a five-and-three-quarter pound cinnamon rabbit hopped over to him. The deadly agent smiled at her.

"Hello Cadbury Alex. I've earned some more money for your trust fund today." He kneeled to rub her head, and she lowered her dark ears. Her coloring stopped part way down her face, and her fur became the same dark color that shaded her ears. The contrasting white spot on her nose distinguished her from show rabbits of her breed and added to her appeal.

Trevor was at peace when he relaxed with his pet. He stopped petting the rabbit. She hopped away a few paces and groomed her face. Cadbury ignored the lingering smell of cordite and went back to lounging on the couch. Trevor checked to be sure Anna didn't neglect to freshen the litter, food, or water. He spotted a note on the table. "I have brushed Cadbury. She is molting. Nails have been trimmed. Anna."

Trevor finished his drink, sat on the sofa next to his pet, and gazed out the oversized sliding glass doors. Although she would stand at the doors or rest on the couch and look into the yard, Cadbury was an indoor rabbit. Trevor had put her on a harness and taken her outside, but she merely stood and looked around. *Maybe Cadbury felt safer indoors, or maybe her room was her territory now, and she was satisfied with the size of her domain?*

Cadbury Alex was very independent for a house pet. She had lived there a little over a year—since she was about a month and a half old. She did seem to welcome the time they spent together though.

Before leaving her alone for the night, Trevor made sure the jo he now used as a doorstop for the sliding door was still in place. His smile widened when he thought of how she had chewed through the yardstick that had been the original stop.

The agent wanted to bathe and go to bed, but first he needed to clean and oil his guns. He gathered the cleaning kit and supplies and took them to the dining room table. He turned on the central fan to help clear the odor.

He stripped the weapons, wiped down the exposed parts on each pistol, and lubricated the barrels. Moments later, the weapons were reassembled. He brought some ammo and a spare magazine upstairs from the basement then worked a round into each chamber and topped off the clips. He put away the cleaning supplies and took the trash out to the garage to reduce the fumes from the stained cotton patches.

While the hot tub filled, he slipped on a pair of swim trunks, made another drink, and grabbed his Colibri lighter and a Baccarat cigar. The bonus he would receive for today's work was a success to celebrate. Instead of settling for the standard ten percent tax-free cut of recovered funds, he had negotiated twenty-five percent on this deal. The water was hotter than he preferred, but it would cool soon since the enclosed room wasn't heated. Before lighting the cigar, he examined the King of Diamonds atop the Nine of Spades on its band. *DOLCE FAR NIENTE.* He rolled the cigar's foot above the lighter and evenly started the end of the Rothschild. He used the lighter's built-in cigar punch to vent the other end then lit the cigar. Mild and touched with a hint of coffee. A perfect cigar, especially with his scotch.

Trevor contemplated his solitary personal and professional lives. *Will anyone remember me if I'm killed? Maybe I should play it safe, transfer to a field office and merely audit financial records? Give up the dangerous, exhilarating occupation that had been so difficult to attain...*

Trevor was pragmatic and knew any mission could be his last. Maybe he was naïve and idealistic, but he would rather risk his life to make an important difference than just catch people misappropriating government funds.

Perhaps he could find another profession that gave him a sense of satisfaction. *Was the samurai whose blade I now possess more fulfilled as a warrior or a monk?* He smirked. *A more relevant question is: will I live long enough to enjoy the wealth I'm building?*

The ice in Trevor's drink had melted. He drained his scotch in one large swallow and flung the stub of his cigar into the empty glass. He opened the hot tub's release, and the water flowed into his yard. He snubbed the remains of his cigar in the sand-filled ashtray near the door and took his empty glass inside.

Trevor shampooed and showered until he could no longer smell the persistent odor of gunpowder. With one SW99 on his nightstand and the other within reach under the unused pillow next to him, Trevor wasted no time falling asleep.

Trevor held his travel mug with what remained of the Gevalia Jamaican coffee he'd made this morning and sat down at his desk. The desk was uncluttered and efficient. His main tools at headquarters consisted of a telephone, computer, and the scanner/printer. The in and out bins were more traditional than functional.

The out bin was empty, and the incoming bin only held a card for him to sign. William Oakes was retiring. When he was younger, he had been called "The Mighty Oak." Now, some of the guys called him "Willie the Willow" behind his back. He looked ancient enough to have built up two pensions instead of one. A full-time desk job in this department came with its own stress and headaches, but odds were the desk jockeys would live to retire. Trevor signed the card with best wishes and tossed it into the out tray. The agent reflected that if a card was issued at the end of his service, it would most likely be a sympathy card. They wouldn't even need to bother since he'd leave no family behind.

Trevor held down the Control, Alt, and Delete buttons, and the login screen requested his password. Incredibly, his agency had only one system that required one user identification and a single password. Unfortunately, to access the myriad other federal agencies and their various databases required a complete list of user IDs and passwords, which he stored in an anonymous document on his PC. Hopefully, the virus protection and firewall were as good as advertised because it would be a nightmare regaining access to every system he utilized frequently if anyone ever hacked into the login information. He keyed in CadBury0405.

While his personal settings were being applied, Trevor hung his black trench coat and his suit jacket on hangers behind the door to his small office. The cherry desk and his leather chair took up most of the room. He wasn't concerned with the size of his workspace. Anything that wasn't already available through the computer could be scanned or downloaded into his PC, and he never interviewed anyone in his office. His area was big enough to house both his office work and his ego.

The desktop image of his rabbit when she was only a few months old was displayed. Trevor opened Outlook and scrolled through the index of public folder forms until he found the current version of the case closure cover sheet. Unlike most government agencies, his employer was realistic. Because Congress felt it had oversight authority anytime it was looking for scapegoats, Trevor's agency didn't create or keep unnecessary documentation. Every time a form was revised, it became shorter, more obscure, or both.

Trevor retrieved Cowen's case number from the system and completed the brief form. He clicked on boxes to indicate "CASE CLOSED—discussed with Case Manager" and "NO report required." He also checked the box directing inquiries regarding deaths or collateral damage associated with the case to the case manager. He emailed the form to his superior with a few more mouse clicks and was ready to open the next file pending in his queue.

Trevor was reaching for his coffee when his phone rang. "Byrne."

"Hey, JB. Andy. Got your message. It's good you called me. I have a great opportunity for you! Listen: I learned a genetics company's doing human testing this Friday for a possible HIV cure. This is big! The stock is only selling for $6.10, but our research department thinks it could go through the roof after the testing."

"Thanks for calling me back, Andy. Within the next few days, my money market will receive another distribution from my uncle's trust fund."

Andy interrupted, "I'd really like to meet your uncle one of these days. I could do good for him like I've been doing for you, you know?"

Trevor quipped, "I've mentioned you to him before, but he says he doesn't need any more money. He's got his own mint."

Andy sighed. "OK, JB. You've got money in motion. What're you thinking?"

"I need $300,000 wired to my overseas account. I want to put another $500,000 into Aurora fund A shares."

"That's three hundred offshore and five hundred in Aurora As. How much are you getting this time? Is that the whole ball of wax?"

Trevor and Andy discussed the $250,000 variable annuity. Andy made suggestions, and Trevor selected one from a well-known insurance company that offered guaranteed living benefits and excellent investment options.

"I'll have my assistant send you the paperwork to sign for the annuity. Hey, JB, with all the money you're worth dead, you really need to find someone to leave it all to. You sure you don't want to meet my younger sister? She's still available, you know?"

"If she looks anything like you, it's no wonder."

"Very funny. I'm serious. If you change your mind, she'd go out with you in a heartbeat. And she likes pets, too."

"Thanks, Andy, but I just wanted to talk about finances today. Oh, what was that 'hot tip' you started to tell me about?"

"Here's the deal. It's risky, but I added this to my portfolio, you know? You can download the prospectus if you want. The symbol is DNAY, trades on NASDAQ. If you have an extra $61,000 on top of what we just did, this is where it should be. It will help balance your portfolio to your objectives, and it's set to soar."

Trevor pulled up DNAY on the quote system Andy's brokerage company provided. "I see your research reports. Andy, I don't trust these gene factories. You see these places testing, failing, and busting all the time. Look at the management. What experience do they have in this field?"

"JB, hate to do this. Another client's holding. I've

got to take her call. You in?"

"I think I'm throwing money down the toilet, but I could use a tax deduction. Put me in for one hundred shares. I want to sell it all if it drops to $3.50 or goes up to $30."

"You got it, JB. You should've picked up more, but you made a smart move. Later."

Trevor hung up the phone and finished his coffee. The first file pending had an urgent flag next to it. He opened the file and leaned closer to the screen. Coincidence? He didn't believe in coincidence.

Trevor's next assignment was to determine how an unknown gene company that only recently went public obtained expedited FDA approval to test an HIV process on human subjects. *"Karl Joseph, CEO, President of Research and Development at DNAY is suspected of illegally obtaining FDA approval for this testing. Investigate DNAY, Karl Joseph, and FDA authorization. Report findings to Executive Case Manager via Case Manager. This is only an investigation, and no punitive action shall be authorized below the level of Case Manager."*

The Good Doctor

Trevor took the elevator to the basement and walked to his parking space holding his overcoat. He hit the button on the key ring to unlock the door and threw his coat on the passenger seat before lowering himself into the Porsche.

The engine turned over more readily than Trevor's first girlfriend and made a much more satisfying sound. The agent plugged the battery charger into his cell phone. Once out of the garage, he made the necessary calls to pressure the right person into adding an appointment in the right calendar.

The silver Porsche entered the Food and Drug Administration facility with time to spare. Unfortunately, it was so vast and the signage so inadequate that Trevor was late when he walked into his meeting with the Acting Director of the Division of Cellular and Gene Therapies.

The office was easily four times the size of Trevor's. Bookcases crammed full of reference journals lined two walls. A refrigerator and small sink adjoined a private bathroom. "Good afternoon, Doctor Singh." The first thing Trevor noticed about the doctor was his small physique. The second was the overpowering stench of a cologne he didn't recognize. Shaking hands with the balding Indian, he apologized, "Sorry I'm late, sir."

"Mr. Byrne, please have a seat. Anything to drink?" Trevor shook his head. "No?" The doctor walked behind his impressive mahogany desk. It was not cluttered by the telephone, large plasma monitor, and keyboard that sat there. "What is three minutes in the overall scheme of things? I'm sure both of us waste much more time than that daily on mundane bureaucracy." The doctor leaned forward and smiled. "You know, the first time I came here I thought I should have minored in cartography. Trying to find the right block on the maps around here...bah." He leaned back in his leather chair. "It was made very clear that you wanted to see me today. What can I do for you?"

Trevor's sinuses were drying quickly from the powerful cologne. He pinched the end of his nose to try to keep his nostrils moist. Although the doctor seemed rather social for someone in his position, Trevor decided to be blunt. "DNAY." He waited for a response. No reaction. None. "Your division approved human testing for an HIV treatment."

Finally, Doctor Singh leaned forward. "Oh yes. DNAY. You should see what they've done. It could be a breakthrough. They may have found the cure."

Trevor pulled out a handkerchief and dabbed at his nose. His throat was becoming raw and irritated. So was he.

"Are you sure you wouldn't like a drink, Mr. Byrne?"

"Water would be fine." He accepted the glass and drank deeply. "Thanks. Now tell me, why was

DNAY's application approved so quickly?"

"Our mission is to promote and protect the public health. We help safe and effective products reach the public in a timely manner. You could have learned that from our web site and saved yourself a trip although I am pleased to have met you."

Trevor set the heavy glass down. "Come on, Doctor. That application was approved faster than most people can decide what to have for dinner. Why?"

The scientist leaned back. He took several deep, calming breaths and said something that sounded like, "...neti neti..." Trevor waited. "Mister Byrne. May I be frank, or will you use what I say against me? I want you to give me your word. I feel I can trust you."

"If you're getting some kind of payoff and risking innocent lives, I'll be back for you another day."

"There are certain political forces at work here, who wanted this project green-lighted. They are very powerful, and they have great influence. They can allow me to retire with a pension, or they can end my career."

"Who's going to make the money here?"

The man stood up and crossed his arms in front of his chest. "Find out who owns DNAY stock. Not just the personal holdings. Who are the institutional investors? That may tell you more than I ever could, Mr. Byrne."

The agent stood, ready to acquire fresh air. "You disappointed me, Singh. For a man with your education, you never learned right from wrong or how much cologne to use." He turned to leave.

Doctor Singh called out, "Wait. Please." He sank into his plush seat, and it seemed to swallow him. "Tell me something before you go. What do you know of my life outside of here?" His gesture took in the room, perhaps the entire Health and Human Services facility.

Trevor recited what he had learned during his long drive. "Doctor Lal Singh. Married sixteen years to the same woman. She's Egyptian, but I forget her name. Two children. Your son, Lal the second, was named after you. He's thirteen and plays soccer. Your daughter, Femi, is almost ten. She's a cheerleader. You have a large suburban home and attend your children's extracurricular events frequently. Clean credit history, you carry minimal balances on your credit cards. Your family values and formidable list of degrees made me respect you before I met you."

The Indian scowled. "I love my family. My children. Do you know that both Lal and Femi are names that refer to the concept of love? My family is the most important thing in my life. Now I ask you, how did you know of my family? Hmm? You looked around my office when you entered. There are no pictures on the desk and no children's drawings on the cooler. Even my screensaver reveals nothing. How do you know so much about my personal life, Mr. Byrne?"

"Only took a few phone calls. Remember, I have friends in very high places."

"My point exactly, Mr. Byrne. I'm not afraid of the politicians and what they can do to my career. I could be happy teaching college science." Trevor watched the man come around the desk and stand in front of him. An invisible cloud of perfume followed. "What I could not risk were the threats to my wife and children. You want to protect those who cannot defend themselves. What would you do? And this is not as hypothetical as you may think. I believe I am being watched. They must know you came to see me. Your family could be in danger. What will you do?"

"I don't have a family, Doctor." Trevor attempted to cover the hint of regret in his voice by coughing. "In my profession that can be an advantage." The agent motioned for the Acting Director to return to his seat. "I'm not sure what I'd have done if I were you. I wouldn't put an unsuspecting public at risk, but what is the risk?"

"That's just it. I don't know. They want to do gene-based experiments, but the information they submitted is incomplete. Nothing we could approve under normal operating protocol. I have a collection of colorful charts, data, and hypotheses but no evidence."

"So it could be harmless? Get FDA approval and the stock price goes up. Take the profit, do a few tests that don't produce results, and file bankruptcy. Do you think that's it?"

Doctor Singh shook his head. "I wish I could say that with a clear conscience, Mr. Byrne, but I cannot. The lead scientist at DNAY is Professor Charles

Garrett. He has a substantial background in chemistry and genetics. His ethics are questionable at best. It has even been rumored that Professor Garrett was responsible for creating chemical weapons. Many of his subordinates specialize in both chemistry and genetics as well. What you've suggested could have been accomplished with businessmen starting any type of company. They may not have received as much startup capital as this scientific venture, but they wouldn't have required the level of salary expense either."

"A politically well-connected team of top scientists formed a genetics research company. Using political pressure and terroristic threats, they've obtained FDA approval to experiment on humans. What can they do now that they couldn't do without your ok?"

"They can *legally* use human test subjects in their experiments."

"What are they up to?"

"It's too early to draw a conclusion. Let me give this puzzle some more thought." He nodded his head in determination.

"Call me if you think of anything." Trevor handed Doctor Singh a business card. "You can leave a confidential message if you reach my voicemail. By the way, do you have any Advil?"

The doctor filled the glass and returned with a bottle of generic ibuprofen. Trevor took three pills and finished the water. His head was pounding. "Thanks again."

NIGHTMARES

The white man walked out of the building giving no special attention to the Lincoln LS in the reserved parking space nor to the rugged black man pretending to study his Pocket PC behind its steering wheel.

Rod Steele watched the unknown man sneeze before entering the Porsche. Rod waited several minutes after the sports car pulled out before he turned over the LS's large engine and backed into the lot. There was no need to maintain visual contact. Rod had placed a homing transmitter securely to the chassis of the Porsche as soon as he had confirmation that its driver had entered Doctor Singh's office. With the Lincoln's reserve gas tank filled, Rod could stay within monitoring range as long as necessary.

He picked up his cell phone and held in the button to speed dial his current employer. "Target acquired. He is driving a silver Porsche Boxster S. New York license plate Marty Terrell Walter one four five two. No passengers."

"Excellent. Follow him until further notice. Call me whenever he stops. Am I clear?"

"I hear you. Out." He clipped the phone back onto his belt.

Rod Steele had worked for numerous individuals

and occasionally taken on assignments that had left a bad taste in his mouth. Even so, deep inside his gut, something about this Kraut cracker really bothered him. The money was good, and Rod wasn't worried about being paid. He just couldn't decide what was causing the gnawing sensation under his skin.

He was somewhat contented that he'd only agreed to provide assistance in matters regarding Doctor Singh's visitors. Whatever else went down wasn't his concern. At least, that's what he tried to tell himself. He pushed aside thoughts of the gasoline tanker.

Lal Singh waited for his wife to answer the phone. The answering machine picked up. "Subira, it is five thirty, and I am preparing to come home now. I will see you and the children soon." He must have been distracted by the agent's visit because he'd already hung up before he realized that he forgot to say he loved her. He would just tell her when he arrived.

He packed some files and CDs that he planned to review after dinner into his black attaché case, closed the latches, and dialed the combinations back to zero. Anyone who knew his anniversary would easily be able to unlock it, but at least the overstuffed briefcase wouldn't pop open and scatter the documents.

He put the briefcase in the back of his gold Lexus LS430 sedan, settled into the luxurious leather driver's seat, buckled up, started the engine, and turned on his headlights. The engine seemed to skip a beat, and the lights blinked off then immediately came back on. The engine resumed its quiet rhythm. *Odd. That had never happened before. Perhaps I need to make an appointment for service? It's a new car. I shouldn't have any problems with it so soon. I will be home in about an hour depending on traffic. I'll wait and call the dealership tomorrow.*

Andre Slaughter looked at the high-tech transmitter with distaste. It was about the size of a portable CD player, with a red toggle switch on the left, a green toggle on the right, and a telescopic antenna that was aimed toward the gold Lexus. Andre had to use it. He didn't have a choice. As soon as his target had started his car, Andre flipped the red power toggle to the on position. When the signal reached the Lexus' engine, it momentarily interrupted the factory-installed computer program and installed a patch. Andre tensed when he saw the lights blink off, but he started breathing again when the lights came back on, and the target pulled out of his reserved parking space.

Doctor Lal Singh was a man of habit. Such men were easy to track and even easier to kill. Andre knew the route the doctor would take to his home. His BMW 525 quickly passed the Lexus, and he started putting distance between them. He had about fifty minutes to get into position. He pressed a button on his CD player and the Thelonious Monk Quartet and John Coltrane played an impressive 1957 Carnegie Hall jazz performance.

* * * *

The gold Lexus turned off the newer state route and onto the original route that now led past strip joints and massage parlors. Although a longer distance, the lack of traffic made it a shortcut to the Singh residence.

Lal was accelerating when he noticed a large truck stopped at the far intersection of the on-ramp, straight ahead.

The tanker truck was in position, and the gold Lexus was in sight. Andre put down his binoculars and flipped the green toggle.

The device transmitted computer instructions to override the Lexus' steering and cruise control systems. Andre set the device down and carefully grabbed a remote detonator that looked like a black cigarette lighter topped with a red button.

Andre picked up the binoculars and focused on the side of the gasoline tanker nearest the Lexus. His assignment was nearly complete.

Lal pressed down as hard as he could, but the brakes didn't respond. Instead, the car actually accelerated. He could read the gasoline company's logo on the side of the tanker as it loomed directly in his path. He tried to turn the steering wheel, but it was locked in place as though the ignition key hadn't released the steering lock.

He reached down to the key but was too late to shut off the engine. The gold sedan rushed into the side of the tanker at seventy miles per hour.

A split second before the collision, Andre depressed the plunger. The doctor's car slammed into the truck at the same moment the huge fuel tank exploded. The fireball engulfed both vehicles. Andre felt the heat reach his position in the parking lot of an abandoned metal shop. *He's toast*. Andre stashed the electronic equipment and the binoculars in his gym bag and drove away. It was getting late, and he wanted to spend some time with his girlfriend before she decided to do something without him.

Rod called to report the stop the man made for coffee and another when the man grabbed a quick meal and went into the restroom. The man was driving into a residential area, so Rod dropped back even farther. It was dark, and Rod didn't want the man to notice his headlights. The Porsche was well within range of the transmitter. The tracking device beeped, and Rod noticed the Porsche had stopped. He pulled alongside the curb and waited a few minutes. No further movement. The target must have reached his destination.

The black Lincoln turned onto the last street the Porsche had taken. Rod paused at the corner long enough to confirm with his tracking device where the Porsche had parked. The fourth house on the right, the one made from stone. Attached two-car garage. Well-lit walk-up landing in front. Open. No large trees or shrubs to use for concealment. From Rod's assessment, he determined the owner was a professional and should not be underestimated. Rod turned at the next intersection, pulled to the curb, and called in another report.

The cold voice on the other end of the phone pierced the low heat Rod was circulating through the car. He almost turned the climate control to a warmer setting, but the momentary discomfort passed. "Wait until you believe him to be asleep. If he is with anyone, take a hostage. Maybe it will loosen his tongue. I want to know who he is, why he visited the doctor today, and what he suspects. Did he tell anyone? Learn all you can. Then kill him. Am I clear?"

"Yeah. Got it. Anything else?"

The Kraut responded violently, "I think of everything and leave nothing to chance! Am I clear?"

"You're clear. Out." Rod set his phone to silent mode and placed it in the Lincoln's glovebox.

Rod turned his headlights off and drove once around the block to get a feel for the layout. He turned back onto his target's street and parked at the corner on the opposite side of the street from his objective.

He shut off the engine, put the keys in the storage area, and then lowered the armrest so the keys would not be visible. The number pad above the door handle would allow access to the car without the risk of his keys clinking and giving him away.

Soon all the lights in the house were off. Rod checked his watch and waited forty minutes. He saw no other activity during that time and determined his target was asleep.

Rod exited the car smoothly and stood to his full height of six feet three inches. If he had not kept his head shaved, he would have been six four. At two hundred fifty pounds, he was mostly muscle and didn't need the extra inch to intimidate people. Rod patted himself to be sure all his weapons were in place. The weapons, ammo, and gear added to his bulk. He closed his eyes momentarily and took a deep breath, visualizing the entry, assault, interrogation, and conclusion. He didn't want to think of it as murder. Rod was satisfied that he was ready for the encounter. He confidently walked over to Trevor's home as though an expected guest.

In the dark of night, Rod was certain no one had seen him approach the home. Without breaking stride, he walked past the front porch, staying outside of its circle of light, and continued along the building until he found the back door. His eyes were already adjusting to the night, but he took out a slim flashlight and shined its beam on the door. He saw both a keyhole in the knob and a deadbolt a few inches above. He tried the knob. It turned. He only had to get past the deadbolt.

Rod reached into his jacket and pulled out a thick cloth containing his lock picks. He chose the rake and the tension tool and had the deadbolt unlocked in under two minutes. He wrapped the tools securely with the cloth and returned the kit to his jacket. He opened the door as silently as possible and waited.

He heard no indication of an alarm. Sweeping the flashlight beam around the door frame, he saw no contact points and knew no alarm system was installed.

The intruder stepped inside and closed the door behind him. Rod drew the 1911 .45 caliber handgun from under his left shoulder. There was nothing to see in the kitchen, so he made his way into the dining room.

He had worked his way through most of the first floor when he went back to the one room that had a closed door. Rod slipped the flashlight into a pocket and turned the knob. He could hear only his own soft breathing. He pushed the door open while standing aside in case of attack. After waiting another thirty-five seconds, he grabbed the flashlight and locked the backs of his wrists against one another to steady his gun hand and illuminate the area. He leaned in and was surprised to see another door just a few feet farther ahead. Suspecting a trap, he recoiled and leaned against the door jamb. The only way to open the next door would be to stand in the narrow space between the doors. If someone was waiting on the other side, it would be easy to shoot the trespasser in this kill zone. The homeowner would be justified citing self-defense. Rod might not be able to completely eliminate the odds against him, but he could certainly cut them down to make them more acceptable.

Rod leaned back and determined that the next door opened away from him, to his left. Rather than walk down the center of the passage, Rod pressed himself as closely to the left side of the short hallway as possible. Tucking the light under his right arm, he grasped the door's handle with his left hand. He thrust the door open then forced himself against the wall and took a deep breath. Rod took the flashlight back with his free hand and again locked his wrists, so the gun and light pointed in the same direction. Hearing movement in the next room, he dropped to a crouch and crept into the room, handgun first.

Rod saw a rabbit dash into the beam of light, look at him, and thump its back legs twice on the floor in fright. The rabbit stared at him momentarily and raced to a hiding spot. It was too late to stop the warning noise that echoed throughout the house. If the owner heard, he would be down soon. If not, Rod would resume his search in ten minutes. Scrutinizing the room, he detected no potential danger. Rod turned off his flashlight and made himself comfortable on the couch.

Trevor normally was a light sleeper, but tonight he had fallen into a deep sleep almost as soon as he had climbed into the queen-sized bed. When he was on assignment and not making any headway, he had nightmares. Tonight was no exception. He was being audited by a rookie IRS agent with something to prove when Cadbury's warning thumps forced their way through his dreams.

The agent remained still and cleared his head as he fought the sleep that threatened to overtake him.

With the airlock closed, he should not have heard Cadbury so clearly. *What would she be afraid of? Something outside her room? Someone inside her room?*

Trevor grabbed the SW99 from the cherry nightstand. Although there was not enough light to visually inspect the weapon, the SW99 was designed so the indicators could be read tactually as well. The agent examined the side and back of the slide by touch. He confirmed a round was chambered, and the striker was in single action mode. Now awake and alert, both he and the pistol were ready.

Staying to the outside of the stairway, he reached the first floor without any of the boards creaking and revealing his descent. A quick check of the first floor revealed nothing out of place except the open airlock doors. If the intruder had remained in the house, he was in Cadbury's room.

Trevor leaned around the nearest door's frame and peered into the darkness of the airlock. For the first time, Trevor recognized the potential deathtrap that short, narrow space formed. Hoping to surprise the trespasser, the agent rolled head over heels through the passage. He rose to a crouch, sweeping the room with his weapon. It settled on a figure much more imposing than the IRS agent he had dreamt about minutes ago.

SURPRISE ATTACK

The large black man turned on his flashlight and slowly rose from the couch, keeping his 1911 trained on the homeowner's chest. "Put the gun down nice and slow." Trevor complied. "Good. Now turn on the light, come over here, and have a seat." He motioned to the couch with his bald head as he moved far enough away to be sure his adversary would not be able to make an unexpected attack. The agent turned on the overhead light. Seeing only one intruder, Trevor asked, "Who are you?" before he sat on the couch.

The formidable black man with the gun shook his head. "You don't need to know who I am." He put the flashlight away and kicked the useless Smith and Wesson to the far corner of the room. "However, I do need to know who you are."

Trevor glanced around the room and saw Cadbury watching the two of them. The rabbit didn't seem to be afraid now, only interested. "I'm Trevor Byrne. If this is a robbery, take what you want and go. I won't try to stop you."

The intruder smiled a disarming, friendly smile. "I don't want your toys. I have my own. What I want is for you to answer some questions." Trevor shrugged his shoulders and opened his arms in a 'why not' gesture. "Good. Now tell me, Trevor. Why did you see that doctor at the Food and Drug Administration today?"

Trevor needed the big man to become accustomed to Trevor's moving around. Perhaps he'd have enough time to go for his opponent's gun. He moved his left arm as if trying to read his watch then realized he was not wearing one. "What time is it?"

The muscular man growled and leveled the weapon at Trevor's face, "Don't ask me any more questions! Am I clear?" Trevor wasn't sure why, but for a fleeting moment after the man asked his question, it looked as though he was disgusted with himself for some reason. The moment passed, and the man looked as menacing as ever.

Trevor noticed Cadbury approach the bald man, sniffing the man's shoes and pant legs with curiosity. The agent didn't want to draw any attention to her. He wanted her to hide somewhere, preferably in another room of the house. Trevor shifted in the seat, so he was balanced and ready to pounce if the opportunity arose. Pretending to focus directly on the intruder's eyes, he answered, "I wanted to get inside information to make profitable stock trades. You know, buy or sell before a big announcement. No such luck. That little guy was tougher than he looked."

Keeping his focus on the seated agent, the big man aimed the gun at the rabbit's head. "No more lies. I'm sure you can imagine what a .45 hollowpoint at this range would do to a seven pound pet." The muzzle moved in her direction, and Cadbury smelled the cordite. The rabbit rubbed her nose with her front paws. Trevor saw his pet tense as her paws returned to the floor and, inexplicably, the thought crossed his mind that she might be offended because the man had overestimated her weight.

Trevor threw up his hands and shouted, "OK! Don't hurt her, I'll talk." The gun was tracking back to him when Cadbury leapt.

Trevor saw his rabbit bite into the vein of the powerful man's wrist, and Trevor bounded from the sofa. The intruder managed to hold on to the gun and snapped his right arm hard enough to send the rabbit flying feet first into the wall near Trevor's discarded handgun. Trevor tried to immobilize the man's gun hand while delivering an uppercut. He didn't have time to see what had happened to his pet but shouted, "Cady, run!"

The big man shook his head to clear it and struggled to pull his right arm free. Trevor grabbed the gun's slide near the muzzle and pushed it away from himself. Trevor tried to pry the gun from his enemy's grasp. The black man was too strong. Trevor saw the man prepare to strike. Maintaining his grip on the gun, Trevor centered his balance and turned his entire body away from the blow. The impetus from the agent's maneuver created enough leverage to force the 1911's barrel toward the back of his opponent's hand. The firearm discharged harmlessly as the intruder's now-broken index finger depressed the trigger. The pistol came out of the big man's hand, but Trevor had to release his own grip to avoid injury from the slide as it cycled to eject the spent casing and load the next round. He realized the gunshot would alert the neighbors, and police would soon be dispatched.

By the time Trevor had recovered the 1911 and aimed it at his attacker, the big man had already pulled his other 1911 from under his right shoulder. Its muzzle pointed menacingly at Trevor's upper chest. Trevor saw his opponent's finger tighten on the trigger and was thankful the man was holding a double action only pistol. A single action gun probably would have discharged with that much tension on the trigger. "Dammit! I came here for answers, and you're gonna give 'em to me!"

The federal agent kept the 1911 he'd obtained trained on the brawny trespasser but slowly angled his body sideways to present a smaller target. "Who sent you?"

"I pull this trigger, and it's all over little man," the black man threatened.

"Put the gun down, and we'll talk."

"Man, the only thing I'm putting down is you." The intruder held his gun steady and reached for his belt with the injured right hand.

Trevor backed up a step and ordered, "Don't move, or I'll shoot!" Trevor knew there was still plenty of time before the police would arrive in response to the gunshot. If Trevor fired, the other man would most likely shoot him too. The agent flinched as the hilt of a knife sailed a mere inch past his face.

The intruder moved with amazing speed for a man of his bulk. His damaged hand clamped Trevor's wrist with so much force that Trevor involuntarily dropped the .45. Before the man released him, Trevor took advantage of his position and thrust his left knee into his adversary's groin. As his large foe brought both hands down to protect himself, Trevor swept the man's legs out from behind.

The unidentified man went down hard, and Trevor kicked his left shoulder. The black man swung his arm and fired instinctively. For a shot that was not aimed, it was dangerously close. The lamp behind Trevor exploded. The agent crushed his heel into the inside of the black man's wrist as hard as he could, pinning it to the floor. His enemy grunted and released the weapon.

Trevor leaned over to retrieve the pistol, but his opponent slammed both of his meaty fists into the agent's back, and Trevor pitched forward. Using the momentum to his advantage, Trevor rolled and came up facing the sliding glass doors. He saw the jo that he'd placed in the track to stop someone from forcing the door open from the outside. He grabbed the wooden weapon and turned to face his opponent.

The intruder had grabbed the nearest 1911 and was in the process of standing. Trevor ran across the room and brought one blunt end of his stick down against the black man's wrist. Bone shattered, and the gun fell to the floor. Trevor pulled the near end of the jo back and spun the staff, so the other end crashed across his enemy's temple. Blood poured from the wound, and the opponent collapsed.

All that training with the jo against a sword must have been useful, Trevor mused. The weapon could even be effective against a gunman at close quarters.

He propped the jo up against the wall and retrieved his SW99. Police sirens pierced the silence, and Trevor took a moment to look around. He didn't see his rabbit. That was a good sign. She was able to hop away and hide during his battle with the intruder. He patted down the fallen man searching for a wallet or additional weapons, rolling him over in the process. Finding nothing, he collected the 1911s and the knife used during their struggle. "Wait here," he instructed the unconscious man.

Trevor walked through the airlock and went to the living room. He placed the confiscated weapons next to the books on his coffee table and concealed his own gun in the drawer of an end table. He opened the door to his landing. A squad car screeched to a halt at an angle in front of his home, blocking the street to through traffic. The officers opened the car doors and crouched behind them—the driver with his service semiautomatic drawn and the other holding the shotgun.

"Some big guy broke into my home and tried to kill me, officers. He's inside, and he's wounded. He'll need medical attention." The driver ordered his partner to radio for an ambulance and cautiously met Trevor at the doorway. "I'm Trevor Byrne. This is my house. I'm a federal agent, and I'm authorized to carry firearms. I have one in there," he pointed to the end table. Before he could continue, the policeman looked around the room and saw the weapons piled on the coffee table.

"What about those?" Without allowing Trevor an opportunity to answer, he asked, "Do you have any identification?"

"Officer, I'm wearing flannel pajamas. Don't you think I'd have dressed if I was going to break into someone's house?" He pointed to the weapons on the coffee table. "And I took those off the prowler."

The policeman was smug. "Well, if this is your home, you should have ID somewhere, right?"

Trevor looked at the name badge. "Officer Dempsey, I have an unconscious man, who may be bleeding to death, in the other room. Let's deal with that situation first, and then I'll go upstairs and get my driver's license and government identification for you."

"Alright, buddy," Officer Dempsey decided to give him the benefit of the doubt—for now. "But don't make any sudden moves. I get an itchy trigger finger at this time of night."

They both turned as they heard a sliding glass door open. Dempsey took a step back, so he could cover both Trevor and the doorway to the room where the sound originated. Trevor shouted, "He's getting away. We've got to stop him." He began to move for the airlock.

Dempsey ordered, "Slowly, buddy. You first."

The agent was fairly certain that his adversary

had no other weapons on him, but what if opening the door was a trick to lure him back into the room? With Officer Trigger Happy behind him, he'd be screwed. Trevor reasoned that the man didn't get the information he'd come for, so he probably was trying to escape. Hoping for the best, Trevor led the officer into Cadbury's room. There were bullet holes in two different walls, blood on the floor, and an open sliding glass door. He hurried to the door and looked out. No sign of the intruder. He was about to run in pursuit when the policeman called out, "I said don't make any sudden moves! Step away from the door!"

The exasperated federal agent slid the door closed, both to keep the cold out and his rabbit in. He sat down on the sofa. "Unless your partner captured him, he's escaped."

"You just stay right there, pal." Dempsey radioed to his colleague, "Did you see anyone leave the house?"

"Negative. What do you want me to do?"

"Take a look around the building. If you see a big guy that's bleeding, cuff him and lock him in the squad car. Otherwise come inside. We need to ask this guy some questions."

Officer Simpson saw a car at the corner start up and back down the road. It turned up an intersecting street and sped away. Officer Simpson came to a sudden realization: he should immediately park the cruiser in the driveway before it caused an accident.

* * * *

Once Dempsey and Simpson finally left, Cadbury came out to check on her owner and her realm. She hopped without any sign of injury. She circled Trevor and sniffed him. The house rabbit went to the bloodstain and stamped her rear legs, obviously not pleased with the blood on her carpet. Trevor didn't want to upset her anymore, so he turned on the central fan to clear the stench of gunpowder. He left the airlock doors open to allow her access to the rest of the house if she desired. He hoped she wouldn't chew through any cords or destroy any carpeting in the other rooms, but after everything she'd been through tonight, he was thankful she was alive.

Trevor had already cleaned his hands as well as he could with the orange scented scrubbing goop, so he reached out and picked up his pet. He examined her carefully. There was no blood, he didn't feel anything broken, and she didn't wince or whimper. She was fine. Thank God! He hugged his pet. Cadbury started to search for an opening, so he let her jump down onto the couch. "Thanks, Cady. You probably saved my life." He reached over. She lowered her head and moved it toward him. He rubbed the top of her nose.

After Trevor cleaned Cadbury's bowl, she hopped over to examine the fresh food he had placed in it and to drink some water. Trevor went to the gun safe in the basement and pulled out another pair of SW99 .45s. The police had impounded all the weapons that weren't locked up as evidence. He checked the action on both guns and loaded the clips using his alternating round method.

Trevor called his case manager to report. He knew Earl would check the caller ID on his home telephone before answering. "Good evening, boss. I was going to wait until morning to tell you how my day went, but it took an unexpected turn."

He heard Earl talking to someone in the background followed by a door closing. "Talk to me."

Trevor explained the situation and the escape of his attacker.

His case manager was concerned and asked, "Do you think there's any chance he crawled away to die?"

The agent replied, "Not this guy."

Earl was busy jotting notes on a legal pad. Soon he'd be typing away on his laptop's keyboard. If anyone matching the intruder's physical description was treated for a broken right index finger, shattered left wrist, and a blunt wound to the left temple at a hospital emergency room, the Justice Department would notify Earl. "I'll get your local police department to back off. Anything else?"

"I think this all happened because I met with Dr. Lal Singh at the Food and Drug Administration today." He summarized the meeting and asked, "Could you have Research investigate DNAY's insider and rule 144 stockholders? I'd like to know who the big investors are and what they are doing: buying, selling, holding? Are any of the major shareowners under investigation? Do politicians or special interest groups have large interests in the company?"

"Do you think the doctor was on to something when he suggested the investors?"

"If he's wrong, Research wastes some time. If he's right, maybe it will help us figure out what they're up to and stop them."

Earl warned, "You are NOT authorized to take corrective action against DNAY, but you might want to pay them a visit. See what falls out if you shake their tree."

"I'll leave first thing in the morning and keep you posted. Sorry to call you at this time of night, sir."

Rod was shaking when he finally stopped the Lincoln. He'd need medical attention soon. How much blood had he lost? His face and jacket were covered with it. He was cold even with the sedan's climate control set for 80 degrees. Before he could contact his private doctor, however, he had another call to make.

He felt vertigo as he leaned over to the glovebox and clutched his phone. With the back of his right hand, he wiped more blood out of his eyes and struggled to keep them open. Resting the injured left wrist on his lap, he used his right thumb to speed dial the Kraut. The icy voice on the other end cleared his senses for the moment. "Report."

"Subject's name is Trevor Byrne. He confirmed that he did meet the doctor. We got into a fight before I could learn more. I'm injured. I barely got away before the police arrived."

"I do not take failure lightly. Do you have anything else to report?"

Rod's temple continued to bleed and his right hand throbbed. He wanted to end this call and speak to his private surgeon immediately. Knowing what he was about to suggest was no longer possible, Rod said, "I recommend you have someone interrogate Doctor Singh. I'm sure he'll talk."

"Mr. Steele, my other operatives have had more success today than you did. The doctor won't be talking to anyone. I suggest you don't either."

The call ended. Rod pressed the 'end' button then speed dialed his surgeon. "I need your attention immediately. Here's where your team can find me..."

FIRST IMPRESSIONS

Trevor sat up in bed when the radio alarm turned on. The WBAL Morning Team were laughing about something, but Trevor shut off the alarm, uninterested in their banter. He sat up in bed and reached behind his back. He winced from the pain. He knew the heating pad would do his back a world of good, but he felt something important was happening with DNAY. The agent's instincts told him losing any time could have disastrous consequences. Besides, Earl wanted him in Middletown, Pennsylvania.

He went downstairs and saw Cadbury at her water bowl. She finished drinking and hopped over to him. The agent leaned down and rubbed her nose while she looked up into his eyes. The room had aired out overnight, so he closed the airlock doors behind him when he went to the kitchen to brew some Gevalia Peruvian coffee.

Trevor booted up his computer and searched for DNAY's address and the directions to get there from his home. The Internet made travel so much easier now than it had been when he first started working for the government. He remembered the days of pulling out road maps to determine the best route. Now, he could just type some data into the computer, and he could find out almost anything he wanted to know. Hell, he could probably find anything at all with the right passwords. He looked over the directions and changed the starting point, so he would follow Interstate 83 North rather than take the local state routes.

He returned the pistols to his safe and then set the shower water as hot as he could stand it. He had to keep wiping steam from the mirror, so he could see to shave. He shampooed, showered, and rinsed. Fortunately, his destination wasn't too far away. He had plenty of time to pack enough clothing to get him through three days and two nights if it became necessary to stay in Pennsylvania.

He pulled on a black tee, buttoned up a burgundy dress shirt, and selected his checkered indigo wool suit. The matching burgundy tie was offset with a gold pattern. Trevor tied it in a half-Windsor knot, and the front stopped just below the top of his belt buckle. He slipped on a pair of the dozen heavy but comfortable black leather Johnston & Murphy Belton penny loafers he owned.

Trevor took a quick look in the mirror. His naturally raven hair was parted just left of center then brushed and blown back. Since he didn't use styling gel, the lock in front fell a little toward his right eye. He pushed it back and smiled briefly.

The final touch was the Seiko watch with silver band and a bezel with gold accents. The steel colored face with gold hour markings went well with most of his suits but especially well with this one. The watch had been a gift from Cindy. Now, the watch, a few photos, and his memories were all that remained of their relationship.

He stuck a handkerchief in the left side pocket of his jacket. Trevor grabbed his wallet, keys, and French blue Waterman pen.

Trevor packed two suits, shirts, and ties; casual clothes for two nights; a supply of underclothes and socks; and his special gear, in case a nighttime penetration was required. He also packed shaving supplies, toothpaste and toothbrush, and a 2.5 ounce bottle of Dolce and Gabbana Pour Homme cologne. He smiled again, wondering how long the small bottle of cologne would have lasted Doctor Singh.

Leaving a quick note for Anna to let her know he might not be home until the weekend, Trevor refilled Cadbury's water and added some rabbit food to her ceramic bowl.

Compared to the recent traveling Trevor had done for his job, the expedition to Middletown, Pennsylvania would be fairly short, but his back was already sore, and he wasn't looking forward to the drive. Besides, he didn't want to waste time determining the best locations in the vehicle to conceal his weapons and holsters. Trevor placed his travel bags in his Toyota Highlander Limited. The Indigo Ink painted SUV was quiet and luxuriously equipped. The leather captain's chair with lumbar support would minimize the trip's impact on his back. Trevor confirmed that his weapons and the spare holsters he kept hidden inside were still secure.

He started the engine and saw he only had half a tank of gas. He turned the heat up, reviewed the directions to his destination, and began the journey north.

The drive up Interstate 83 North was uneventful, and Trevor found he was paying more attention to a self-help book on CD than to the road. He noticed two large smokestacks to his right while he crossed the bridge that took him to the Harrisburg side of the Susquehanna River. Shortly after that, his side of the highway went from three lanes down to two, and he had to slow as traffic began to bottleneck. Then, he was passing some shops that sat on the other side of the concrete barrier to his right. He looked at the green highway signs ahead and saw that he was closer to his destination than he'd realized. As he took the ramp to 283 South, he saw a memorial cross in the pit between the ramp he was on and the road he'd just turned off. *There's no escaping Death. When it's your time, he'll find you anywhere.*

Trevor eased into the turn that promised to take him toward the Airport and Lancaster. He looked over his left shoulder and saw a rapidly closing gap between an old Ford truck and a white Corvette. Trevor adjusted his speed and pulled into the traffic lane directly behind the pickup. The punk in the Corvette blared his horn and pulled into the vacant passing lane. Trevor pretended not to notice the one-fingered salute the driver offered as he sped past.

Trevor passed the Swatara, Route 441 exit. He

continued on and saw that he needed the final exit ramp or else he'd end up on the Pennsylvania Turnpike. He flipped his turn signal to indicate that he wanted to get over soon. A stream of vehicles was entering the road ahead of the Ford truck with no indication that the drivers had seen the yield sign at the end of the on-ramp. Harrisburg wasn't as busy as Baltimore, but the drivers in Pennsylvania all seemed to think that whatever they were doing was more important than being safe and courteous on the road. *Fuck the bastards*, Trevor thought and pulled into the busy lane. Trevor was slightly amazed to see the person he had cut off was adept enough to honk the horn, raise his fist, and hit the brakes at the same time.

Trevor looked across the highway as he took the sharp turn. He saw the Turnpike Administration Building with several flags flying at full mast. Next, he noticed a fast food restaurant adjacent to a Handi Hotel. *I should stay there if I need to stay in the area,* Trevor decided. He entered the highway without incident and paid close attention to the signs.

He saw a sign stating the 441 South, Harrisburg International Airport exit was only one mile ahead. Another advised taking the next exit to reach Penn State at Harrisburg. He passed another sign for the Airport, now only a half mile away, and saw a white barn to his right with a large star on the side. The roof, as well as the barn itself, appeared to be in disrepair. Below the star facing the highway was a banner asking for help saving the Star Barn and a website address.

Trevor took the exit ramp at a few miles an hour faster than the posted 35 mile per hour suggested speed limit. If he stayed in the lane he was in, he would go to the airport. Trevor turned into the right lane that was an offshoot of the on-ramp. He obeyed the stop sign at the top of the hill and then turned left onto Spring Garden Drive. He'd only driven a short distance before turning left at the first intersection to take 441 North.

He had the green light and drove through the intersection where a convenience store and gas station sat. A farm was to his left, and Trevor realized that this entire area had probably been farmland in the not-too-distant past. He slowed at the next intersection and saw it was Kreider Drive. He turned right onto Kreider and slowed.

The brick and glass DNAY research facility was visible but sat back a good distance from the road. Trevor entered the driveway and reconnoitered his surroundings. Unlike Cowen's fortress, the DNAY parking lot was only a relatively short distance from a busy highway. He drove to the rear of the building and saw that only one road led into and out of the site. At its rear, he saw a loading dock with a metal door. Next to the dock was a secured entrance and keycard reader. A small flight of concrete stairs led from the security door to the macadam. An industrial dumpster sat across from the dock.

He returned to the front of the three-story building without observing any entrances or exits other than the rear security door and the main lobby doors. There were none of the usual signs of a basement: no windows at ground level and no stairs leading down. The shatter resistant windows would not open, at least without using some C-4 or heavy firepower. He noticed a black Mercedes limousine and the sign reserving that parking space for CEO Karl Joseph. Trevor found an open visitor parking space near the front door and backed the Highlander into the spot. Trevor preferred to park so he could pull straight out if he needed to leave in a hurry. He exited the vehicle and pressed the button on his keychain remote to lock the SUV and arm its alarm.

From the outside, the facility seemed perfectly normal. Trevor approached the automatic sliding glass doors and adjusted the knot in his tie. The doors opened silently for him. As he walked into the foyer, he noticed panels on the walls on each side. So, DNAY screened all its guests for weapons, probably an antiterrorist measure. It was a good idea to take precautions with the world political climate what it was these days. Trevor was glad he had left his weapons in his SUV. Although he didn't like to be too far away from his guns, he knew from experience that it was much easier to meet with corporate executives if they thought he was defenseless.

Trevor noticed a burly young man in a sport coat and tie at the reception counter across the vast lobby. The navy blazer with gray slacks, white shirt, and matching navy tie were polyester blends. The inexpensive, but easy to care for, clothing created the effect of a guard's uniform rather than a professional business ensemble. The sport coat was too snug to button, and the way the man's short arms hung at his sides reminded Trevor of an ape or maybe a professional wrestler. This man's first concern would be security, not finding a better tailor or customer relations.

The young man smiled and nodded, "Good afternoon, sir. How can I help you?" Trevor pegged him as originally being a Boston native. It was funny how in some areas of Boston everyone seemed to have the same accent as this man, but just a few miles away nobody did.

Trevor looked at the nameplate on the desk. "Good afternoon, Anthony. My name is Trevor Byrne. I'm here to see Mr. Joseph."

Anthony glanced at his desk and replied, "You don't seem to have an appointment, Mr. Byrne. Mr. Joseph is extremely busy. May I tell him why you are here, and I'll ask if he would like to see you?"

The speech was slow but polite and distinct. Trevor's estimation of Anthony rose to somewhere above a typical ape or wrestler. More of a loyal lapdog perhaps? Trevor flashed his identification and badge. He stated bluntly, "I'm a federal agent, and I need to talk to him about how your company obtained questionable FDA approval for human testing." He folded his leather ID case and returned it to his jacket's left breast pocket.

Although nobody else was within hearing range, Trevor's reply seemed to have the desired effect. The guard's eyes narrowed, the veins in his neck bulged, and his face reddened. He tersely ordered, "One moment." Anthony picked up the phone and pressed one of its many buttons. "Mr. Joseph, it's Mr. Virelli at Reception. I am sorry to bother you. Trevor Byrne is here to see you. He is a government agent and would like to discuss what he called 'questionable FDA approval.'"

Anthony listened for a moment and nodded. "Very good, sir. I'll let him know." He replaced the receiver. "Mr. Byrne, Ms. Flynn will be down shortly to escort you. Would you like to have a seat?" he asked as he motioned to some antique chairs that looked like they would be very comfortable.

"Yes, thank you, Anthony." Trevor had only been seated for a minute or two when a woman arrived in the corridor behind the reception desk.

Trevor watched discreetly as she walked across the atrium. Her short violet skirt could barely pass for business length and, paired with the matching stiletto pumps, showcased her long, well-toned legs. It was difficult for him to move his eyes off them to see how the rest of her looked. The low-cut ivory chemise was worn under an unbuttoned jacket and emphasized her generous bosom. Her red hair was teased and fell more than halfway down her back. Having observed over the years that most redheads were busty—ever since he was a teen and saw a new wave album cover with an attractive redhead reclining on the hood of a car, in fact—he decided that both the hair color and breasts were natural.

Trevor was disappointed she didn't lean forward when she asked, "Mr. Byrne?" He suspected the guard behind her was disappointed as well. Finally, he met her gaze. He was stunned. Not only did she have an incredible body, but her face was a finely chiseled oval with high cheekbones, full pink lips, and the most beautiful green eyes he'd ever seen.

Trevor smiled and stood to shake hands with her. "Please, call me. I'm Trevor. I mean, please call me Trevor. And you're Ms. Flynn?"

"You can call me Lyn," she smiled back.

"Did I get that right? You're name is Lyn Flynn?"

She laughed, and he was smitten. "Actually, it's Lynda Flynn, but my friends all call me Lyn. Follow me." He didn't care where she went; he knew he could follow her anywhere.

She walked to the elevator, and Trevor saw the way her hips swayed with each step. "So, you're some kind of secret agent?" she asked in her husky voice.

He laughed, "I work for the government, but it's no secret. What do you do here?"

"I'm Mr. Joseph's executive secretary. I handle all of his work that he doesn't have time to do personally."

They walked past the public elevators and to the private car at the end of the hallway. She swiped a keycard, and the door opened immediately. Trevor wasn't sure how much time he had left alone with her, so he decided to be bold and make his move now. "Lyn, would you want to get together after work some day soon? I'd like to learn more about you."

She turned and handed him one of her business cards. She must have had it ready before he'd asked because he didn't see her reach into a pocket to get it. "This week is bad for me, between Thanksgiving and work, but call me and we could get together next week." He looked at the card to be sure it was hers and then carefully placed it in his wallet.

The elevator doors opened onto the third floor, and Lyn was back to business again. "Mr. Joseph will meet with you in his conference room." She led him into the spacious room. There was a round table composed of four curved mahogany sections surrounded by twelve chairs like the ones in the atrium below. A service bar equipped with alcoholic beverages as well as coffee and water stood to one side, and a projection screen lined another wall. The large windows overlooked the parking lot. There was no artwork in the conference room. No telephones either. Trevor realized the room was most likely soundproof and frequently swept for listening devices.

Trevor went to the nearest window to confirm his orientation within the building. As he'd thought, the conference room overlooked the front parking lot. He saw a broad-shouldered black man in dark clothes kneeling at the rear of his Highlander. Trevor narrowed his eyes for a better look. *Was that the same man who tried to kill me last night? No. This one has hair. Short, but so short, it must be natural. Not part of a disguise.* When the man stood, Trevor saw that he was not as tall as the man who had attacked him. "You have an excellent view of the parking lot from here at the top."

"Ha! There's nothing to look at. You can't see the Star Barn or even TMI from here."

"I passed the Star Barn on the way here. Looks like it's seen better days. What's TMI?"

Lyn looked as though she was surprised by the question. "Three Mile Island. The nuclear power plant."

"The one that almost melted down in the late seventies! It's nearby?"

She nodded and pointed to the southeast. "Just out that way a bit."

Trevor grabbed the nearest chair to steady himself. He wasn't even aware that he gasped, "My God."

Lyn hurried over to him. "Are you okay? All of a sudden you don't look so good." She helped him into the chair. "Would you like some water or something?"

"Scotch with ginger ale and a slice of lime. Make it a double." Trevor shook his head. "On second thought, coffee. With just a little cream."

She brought his drink, and this time she leaned forward for him. "How's that look?" she asked as she handed him the cup.

Trevor's smile returned when he saw the top of the white bra supporting her round breasts. He looked up into her welcoming green eyes. "Perfect."

"You seem to be better. Call me if you need anything more," she offered and left him alone in the conference room.

"I will," he said to himself. He drank the coffee and cursed his lack of preparation for this assignment.

Trevor had expected to wait for the Chief Executive Officer to arrive and was not surprised when twenty minutes had gone by. He helped himself to more coffee and used the adjoining restroom. Another half hour had passed before the executive joined him. Trevor stood to meet him.

Trevor immediately noticed the way the blond man's piercing blue eyes studied him. Trevor took the opportunity to study his adversary as well.

Karl Joseph was a few inches taller than Trevor. He casually walked into the room as though he had all the time in the world and was making a social call. The well-tailored, custom-made navy pinstripe three-piece appeared to be a cashmere blend. It perfectly draped the man's strapping frame. Besides an exceptional tailor, Karl Joseph had excellent taste. His sophistication was evident from the way he matched the subtly patterned tie and the mint shirt to the suit. "Thank you for stopping, Agent Byrne. Perhaps next time you would extend the courtesy of making an appointment first?"

The men shook hands. Trevor nearly winced at the pressure Karl's large hand applied, apparently nonchalantly. The blond man's hand was smooth but very powerful. The CEO was tall and all muscle. Someone who could more than handle himself in a fight. Trevor said, "I had to be in Harrisburg yesterday and was hoping I could meet you while I was in the area."

"Would you like more coffee? Or something stronger?" Karl asked as he sauntered to the bar.

"I'm fine, thanks," Trevor replied. He waited while Karl poured himself a glass of vodka on ice. Karl politely cupped a hand around the rim of the glass to avoid spraying his guest with any of the juice as he squeezed a slice of lemon into his drink then carefully dropped the slice into the vodka. He picked up the glass and swirled it to mix the drink. Although the executive didn't seem to know his own strength when shaking hands, he didn't spill a drop of his drink.

The executive sat three seats away, closer to the bar than to Trevor. Karl leaned back in his chair and crossed his legs the way a woman would. "Now, why are you here?" Karl looked at the agent the way someone in a bar would look at a possible one night stand. Trevor felt a sudden pang of nausea.

Trevor fought his urge to lean forward confrontationally and instead leaned back himself. "I know you circumvented the Food and Drug Administration's due process and obtained approval for running experiments on humans in a rather less-than-ethical manner. What I don't know is why. Tell me."

Karl maintained his intense presence, yet

somehow seemed aloof and unconcerned about the meeting's outcome. "Agent Byrne, that was quite a mouthful. I'm appalled you would make such an accusation, but rather than have my attorney parry your thrusts, let's speak as men shall we?"

Trevor motioned with his right hand for the executive to continue. Karl pressed his hands flat against the table and leaned forward, like a tiger ready to pounce. Except Trevor had never seen a tiger glare with such brutal blue eyes. "It's very simple, Agent Byrne. The FDA wants to help the citizens of this great country. We here at DNAY believe we have found a way to wipe out both HIV and AIDS, first across the United States and then the world. Do you have any idea what HIV is doing to the people in Africa, Asia, and India, Agent Byrne? We expect to alter the lives of over forty million people who are infected. That does not include the impact on their families and close friends. Not only will we improve the condition of humanity, but we'll have a permanent place in God's Book and future history texts."

"I'm surprised you didn't mention the fortune you stand to make."

"As CEO of this company, it is difficult to say which is more important, improving the human race or making a profit for our stockholders." He laughed briefly at his own joke. Trevor didn't. "Do you have any reason to doubt me?"

Trevor replied, "Just what my gut tells me."

Karl stood. "Well, Agent Byrne, I believe we are

through here. I have important matters to attend."

Trevor moved to interpose himself between the executive and the conference room's door. "How many nuclear physicists do you have on your payroll, Mr. Joseph?"

The CEO looked puzzled. "None. Why?"

Trevor took a step toward the executive. "DNAY is located conveniently close to Three Mile Island. You expect me to believe that's a coincidence?"

Karl smiled. "I assure you, Agent Byrne, what we are doing here has nothing to do with nuclear power."

Trevor extended his hand, prepared for Karl's strong grasp. "Thanks for your time, Mr. Joseph. I look forward to seeing you again."

The executive began walking away but turned back to face Trevor. "That is a pleasure I don't believe you'll have. Please wait here. My assistant will show you out. Good day." The door closed behind him.

Karl Joseph's commanding voice carried through the speaker in his executive secretary's telephone. "Ms. Flynn, Agent Byrne's presence here concerns me. I suspect he would find you attractive. Go out with him tonight and find out what he knows about DNAY. I'll ask you for a full report tomorrow."

Looking at the appointment calendar on her computer she objected, "I have plans this evening, sir. How about—"

The callous response left no margin for uncertainty, "If you value your position here, Ms.

Flynn, you will entertain Agent Byrne this evening. Pump him for as much as you can get out of him. Am I clear?"

She answered, but the connection was severed before she completed her, "Yes."

Lyn walked into the conference room. "How was your meeting with Mr. Joseph?"

"It didn't go as well as I'd hoped."

Lyn's smile dazzled the agent. "Well, I do have some good news. I managed to clear my calendar for this evening. Where would you like to take me?"

CHECKING IN

Trevor climbed into the driver's seat and turned over the SUV's engine. As the vehicle warmed, he pressed and released the command button on his cell phone. At the prompt he said, "Call Handi Hotel." He reserved a room at their nearest location and asked for directions.

Andre Slaughter had been recalled from the Food and Drug Administration after he had eliminated Doctor Singh. He didn't see why the genetics lab needed so many armed security men or why, if their primary purpose was to deter or stop terrorists, they didn't patrol the grounds with their street sweepers. Everything about the safety measures was unusual. The pay was excellent, but that was odd too.

Perhaps the queerest thing of all was Karl Joseph—the CEO himself. From what Andre had gathered, Mr. Joseph was a real hands-on CEO, probably a control freak. Any other detail Andre had been assigned to had a head of security and that was the officer's only function. At DNAY, all of the security detail reported directly to Mr. Joseph. Something about the man made Andre nervous. Mr. Joseph was like a bomb with a timer Andre couldn't see—Andre didn't know when he would explode.

Andre followed the blue SUV at a discreet distance in the older BMW 525. Even with the tracking device attached to the sports utility vehicle, Andre maintained visual contact. He didn't want the driver to head in to the city and pull into a garage without him seeing which one it was. If he lost the trace, he'd be screwed. He didn't want to personally discover Mr. Joseph's response to failure.

He was thankful when the SUV stopped in the parking lot of a nearby Handi. Andre parked the dark gray BMW close enough that he could see the SUV in his passenger's side mirror. Allowing the engine to idle, he called his employer. The voice was cold, even through the tiny speaker. "Mr. Slaughter, the man you are tailing is a government agent named Trevor Byrne. Learn his room number at the hotel. If he leaves, follow without being observed. Report everything. Do not take any action against him and do not make contact with him unless I amend my instructions. Am I clear?"

"Got it. I'll keep you posted." Andre shut off his engine, turning his key to the accessories position. He powered on his car's music system. The soft jazz relaxed him.

Trevor waited at the traffic light. The Handi Hotel sat conveniently across the boulevard. He wasn't surprised that a fast food chain had a restaurant at the corner of the busy intersection. He slowed down as he pulled into the hotel parking lot and was taken aback by the cemetery behind the restaurant. He'd noticed the memorial cross when he turned off the interstate, now the cemetery. Pennsylvania was known to have one of the nation's highest senior populations, but he hadn't expected to be reminded of mortality so frequently. Maybe he just noticed the signs more readily these days.

A gray car was coming up quickly behind him. Trevor turned into the nearest row to his right and parked in the first open spot. He grabbed his travel bags, locked the Highlander, and entered the hotel. A young brunette clerk at the front desk smiled and asked, "Can I help you?"

He smiled back and replied, "Hello. I'm Trevor Byrne. You should have a reservation for me."

"Hi, Trevor. My name's Tiffany." When she pushed her shoulders back, he couldn't help but notice how her black jacket pulled open across her chest. She pointed to her nametag with enthusiasm. Tiffany's hazel eyes glanced up, and he realized she had caught him looking down her loose tan blouse. She licked her lips and continued to flirt, "Let's see if I can get you into a room." She typed his name into the system and giggled. "Room 419. That's easy to remember—I'm 19! I just need a credit card and your driver's license." She pulled out a room key and began to program it.

Trevor realized the young girl didn't have any reservations after all. She brushed his hand while taking the requested items. "You'd better give me two keys, in case my wife and I get separated."

She pulled out another key and playfully asked,

"You don't wear a wedding ring. Are you likely to be separated?" Tiffany placed the registration form on the counter and pointed to the line with his name printed underneath. "I can get off after four."

He signed the form, and she returned his credit card and license. He placed them back in his wallet. "There are a lot of men my age who would gladly take advantage of you, Tiffany. You should look for someone closer to your own age. Someone you'd have more in common with."

She held out the keys and grabbed his hand when he reached for them. "I've been with older men than you. The only complaint I ever heard was this one guy who said he couldn't breathe and thought his chest was going to explode." Still holding his hand, she leaned forward far enough to reveal that she was not wearing a bra under her tan top, and both of her perky breasts had pierced nipples. A single chain of silver with dangling beads ran from one nipple to the other. The red beads accented her dark pink nipples.

"Tiffany, those are very nice and so are you, but I really am meeting someone tonight." Trevor pulled his hand free and took both keys. Trevor rode the elevator to the fourth floor and followed the sign to the right. His room was the second from the end of the corridor along the outside wall. He opened the door, placed his bags on the bed, and familiarized himself with the layout.

Immediately to his right was a bathroom. He walked in and was pleased. It was clean, the towels were fresh, the toiletries were laid out for him, and there were two heavy water glasses, rather than the plastic cups often found at other hotels. There was even a disposable razor and a packet of shaving gel. He saw the closet across from the bathroom and walked over to it. He opened the sliding doors and checked the instructions for using the unlocked safe. It was large enough to store anything he'd want to keep secured during his stay.

The main room had a dresser along the left wall with a color television attached securely atop it. Across from the dresser, the king-sized bed sat against the wall to his right. There was a nightstand to either side of the bed. Between the bed and the window was a round table with two stuffed chairs.

Trevor quickly unpacked his bags. He had plenty of time before his date with Lyn. Rather than use the hotel phone, Trevor opened his cell phone and called his case manager. "Earl, Trevor here. Do me a favor. You know how to get driving directions from the internet?"

"I'm not exactly a Luddite. I just don't trust technology as much as you do. Where are you starting, and where are you going?"

"What's the distance from DNAY's lab to the Three Mile Island nuclear power plant, and how do I get there?"

Trevor heard a sharp hiss of air on the other end of the call. Earl answered, "If you follow 441 southeast, DNAY is only seven miles from Three Mile Island. The drive would take less than fifteen minutes. Don't tell me you've found a connection?"

"There must be one. Why else would they set up shop so close to the reactor?"

"Trevor, some things are just coincidence."

"The Thanksgiving holiday, Earl. They probably have reduced staffing and security at the power plant over the holiday weekend."

"I could arrange additional security. Stop them if they attempt to get in."

"Or we could let them get inside. Then stop the bastards."

"All right, Trevor. I'll take care of it, just in case you're on to something here. What will you do in the meantime?"

"I'm taking a guided tour of the facility. If you can get me a special pass."

Andre knew the man's name. It would be easy enough to learn the number of his hotel room if he'd checked in using his real name.

The cell phone rang, and Trevor looked at the display. He flipped open the phone. "Yeah, Earl. How'd you make out?"

"Their Security Director, Harvey Franks, will meet with you, but he refused to let you look around. You're expected at one. Just present your official ID."

"You've arranged for extra internal security over the weekend?"

"The inside of that plant will be locked down tighter than a roach motel. Terrorists won't check out."

"OK, Earl. I'm going to grab some lunch. I'll check in later."

The agent was about to flip his phone shut, but Earl cut in, "Trevor, be careful. The doctor you met yesterday had an unfortunate accident."

"What happened? Is his family ok?"

"He ran into a tanker truck on his way home from work after you talked to him. Preliminary reports indicate Doctor Singh's death is going to be labeled a homicide. His family hasn't been harmed."

"Earl, can we get them under protective custody?"

"Trevor, it's the day before Thanksgiving. Not everyone is as dedicated to work as you. I'll see if their local boys want some overtime, but I'm not going to promise you anything."

"He told me his family had been threatened. I think we owe it to them."

"I said I'll try. Watch your back, Trevor."

"Always." He flipped the phone shut and left the hotel.

Andre was waiting in the BMW when the government agent walked out of the hotel. The agent looked to his right and then to his left. He paused for a few moments, looking again in each direction. With a look of determination, the agent walked off to his left. He had decided to walk to the taco chain for lunch rather than go to the home of the "plain old hamburger."

Andre waited until Trevor Byrne was out of the

parking lot before he went into the Handi Hotel. The young babe at the front desk wasn't busy, and he walked right up to the counter. "Hi. Anyone ever tell you how good you look in that outfit?"

The girl looked at him and her smile faded. "Yes, sir. All the time. Can I help you?"

He wasn't expecting such a cold welcome. He wasn't wearing enough cologne, he was losing his charm, or she didn't like black folk. He was fairly certain he was still a smooth-talking charmer, and he'd worn enough cologne this morning. He hated people who were prejudiced, especially when they were white, but he needed her at the moment. "Yeah, thanks. I'm here to meet with Trevor Byrne. Has he checked in yet?"

"Yes, sir."

The phone's number pad was visible from where he stood. "Great. Could you call his room for me and tell him Isaac Holmes is here?" Andre asked.

She smirked at the name. "He just left the hotel, sir. I can take a message for him."

"He knew I was in a hurry, and he said he'd meet me here. Damn. I'll have to call him later. What room is he staying in, honey?"

"I'm sorry, sir. That information is confidential. Would you like to leave a message for him, Mr. Holmes?"

Andre looked past the girl to the numbered slots on the wall behind her. "Yeah. Tell him Isaac Holmes was here for our appointment, and he can come to my office if he still wants to meet."

The girl wrote down the message and showed it to Andre. "Is this correct, Mr. Holmes?"

"Yeah. Fine. Thanks." Andre watched her walk to the slots and squinted. *419. Got it!* She came back, and he handed her a five dollar bill. "On second thought, don't give him the message after all. I'll try to catch him later."

She stuck the five in a jacket pocket. "No problem, sir." Andre watched her take the message out of the slot and crumple it. He left the hotel as she tossed the message in a trash bin.

THREE MILE ISLAND

Trevor reached the power plant with a few minutes to spare. He pulled his Highlander to the gate and handed over his government photo identification. "Hello. Federal Agent Trevor Byrne. I have a one o'clock appointment with your Director of Security, Harvey Franks."

The soldier examined the identification and keyed some information into his computer terminal. He returned the identification along with a badge. "Confirmed. Park over there. Mr. Franks will be waiting for you inside. Be sure to display your visitor's badge on your jacket before you enter the building."

The security gates rolled open. Trevor parked in the area by the building the soldier had indicated. He pocketed his official ID and clipped the badge to the front pocket of his jacket.

Trevor looked around as he entered the building. He saw a young man wearing a heavy wool suit and a photo ID badge. The youth looked all of about seventeen years old, five feet four, and maybe one hundred pounds. Then, Trevor saw the large semi-automatic holstered on his left hip. *One hundred and six pounds. With the gun.*

The man approached, and Trevor could now see

the crows' feet around his eyes and the worry lines that furrowed his brow. He glanced at the name on the badge just as the man stuck out his hand. "Harvey Franks. Good to meet you."

Trevor shook his hand. "Trevor Byrne. Thanks for seeing me on such short notice, Mr. Franks."

"Call me Harv. If someone from your office suspects a security threat to this plant, I'll make time. Let's go to my office." Trevor followed the diminutive man. Franks sat behind his desk and motioned for Trevor to sit across from him. "Now, what do you have?"

"Do you typically have reduced security staffing around the holidays, specifically through this weekend?"

"No less than when staff schedule vacations. I appreciate you arranging to have an extra dozen National Guardsmen on duty within the plant from this evening through Monday morning. I'm asking you again, why do you feel it's necessary, Agent Byrne?"

"There's a genetics lab over in Middletown, less than fifteen minutes away. Something's about to happen. I'm not sure what, but my gut tells me it's going down in the next few days, and it involves your nuclear power plant. Why would someone want to do that?"

"What the hell would geneticists know about nuclear physics?"

Trevor leaned into the discussion. "Normally nothing, but something's wrong there. They may have hired enough geneticists to appear legit, but maybe they received special training. I've had experience against terrorists before. If DNAY is a front, you're the nearest high-profile target. If I'm wrong, you've got some pissed off guardsmen getting paid for sacrificing their holiday weekend. If I'm right, you'll have the advantage: you'll already be on alert."

Trevor saw the man's steely eyes dart back and forth as he considered Trevor's question. "Hell, how many scenarios do you want? Worst case is some suicide group taking over and forcing a core meltdown. The devastation to this area and the families living within the danger zone would be horrendous. Of course, a terrorist group could try to take over the plant and threaten a meltdown unless their demands were met, or the environmental wackos might want to take over the plant to demonstrate nuclear power isn't safe. Would you like more?"

Trevor shook his head. "What about a terrorist cell stealing components for a nuclear bomb?"

"A dirty bomb, possibly. Not a nuke."

"What about enriched uranium?"

"Agent Byrne, we can sit on our asses and talk scenarios all day. I'd prefer you go do your job and allow me to do mine." The small man stood and looked down at Trevor.

The agent remained seated. "I'd like you to show me around the plant and the island. Let me —"

"Thank you for sharing your hunch with me,

Agent Byrne. I'll handle things from here."

Trevor stood and studied the man for a moment then extended his hand. "You seem to be on top of everything. Thanks for your time, Harv."

On his way back to the Handi Hotel, Trevor called his office. "Earl, it's Trevor. I've just left Three Mile Island."

"And?"

"Franks knows his job. That end's covered."

"What's your next move?"

"I'm having dinner with Karl Joseph's executive secretary, Lynda Flynn. I'll learn whatever I can from her."

"Keep me posted. By the way, the Vice-President called to commend you for your recent work in L.A. He's pleased you're still alive and on active duty."

"Thanks for telling me, Earl. I'm just glad things turned out the way they did." Trevor ended the call.

Trevor had some time before he needed to meet Lyn, so he returned to his hotel and borrowed a laptop. He scanned site after site researching DNAY's corporate profile, mission statement, and other corporations in the same sector. The more he read the less certain he became about Karl Joseph's interest in Three Mile Island. He could tell the scientists had spent considerable time specializing in genetics. They would have had little time to learn nuclear physics.

He lost track of time as he considered the problem. *What the hell are they planning to do?*

PASSION

If he was going to pick up Lyn punctually, he'd have to hurry. There was no time to shave. He took a hot shower, toweled briskly, blew his hair dry, and then sprayed some Dolce and Gabbana Pour Homme cologne on his chest.

After wearing a suit and tie all day, he wanted to wear something more casual this evening, but the restaurant Lyn mentioned earlier sounded like a suit and tie affair. At least he had fresh clothes for the evening out. The silver in his patterned tie went well with the gray shirt and looked sharp when he matched it with his black suit.

Trevor felt the bite of the cold air as he walked to his Highlander. He started the engine to warm the vehicle, but he also wanted to be able to leave immediately if the need unexpectedly arose.

He looked around out of habit and noticed that the dark gray BMW across the lane was now idling. The German auto was discharging wisps of exhaust into the cool breeze. Trevor hadn't seen anyone enter the vehicle immediately before or after he'd reached his SUV. Looking more closely, he could see that the man seated in the BMW seemed to be paying a lot of attention to his far outside mirror, especially considering his car wasn't even in reverse yet. Trevor didn't recognize the black man by what he could see of his face in the small mirror. He decided to keep an eye on the sports car while he finished dressing for his evening out.

Since he would be meeting his date in the DNAY parking lot, he didn't need to consider the metal detectors inside the DNAY entrance. In addition to the weapons hidden in his SUV, Trevor always kept both a shoulder holster and an inside the waistband holster stored in the vehicle. He removed his jacket and placed it on the passenger seat. With all the practice he'd had over the years, it wasn't difficult to put the holsters on inside the vehicle. The shoulder holster went on easily over his shirt. Trevor lifted himself in the seat, stuffed his inside the waistband holster into his slacks, and secured its clip to his thick belt. He put the jacket back on and pulled the cuffs of his shirt sleeves, so they were visible.

Keeping his weapons out of view of possible passersby, Trevor inspected each handgun in turn. He looked down over the top of the slide. The loaded chamber indicator angled inward to reveal the red dot, confirming a round was chambered. He ejected the magazine and verified it was at its nine round capacity. The top round was a law-enforcement-only armor-piercing bullet, as expected. He shoved the clip back into the frame until it clicked into place.

The striker was decocked, the pistol ready and waiting in double action mode for the first shot to be fired. Once the initial shot was taken, the slide would cock the striker into single action position for the following rounds. The lighter trigger pull allowed more rapid and, for some users, more accurate shooting after the weapon was engaged.

Trevor kept his thumb on the rear of the slide as he holstered the pistol under his shoulder. It was a safety precaution he'd learned years ago. If the striker pin started to push out, it was an urgent warning that the trigger was moving and to stop holstering the gun immediately before accidentally shooting himself or someone else.

He repeated the process with the other firearm. Satisfied, he stuck that pistol in the black leather holster nestled against the shirt at the small of his back. Now that he was armed, he felt more comfortable, except for the occupied BMW that continued to idle across from him. He noted it had Pennsylvania plates and memorized the number using a mnemonic memory tool. Big Bertha Eats thirty or thirty-five times a day.

Although it would take him the long way through the parking lot, Trevor pulled out of his parking spot and turned left. As he turned into the traffic lane, he glanced toward the driver of the German car. The man looked back at him then jerked away. He suddenly became very interested in something in the opposite direction. Trevor wasn't completely positive, but suspected it was the man he'd seen kneeling by his Highlander when he'd looked out the window in DNAY's conference room.

Had Trevor noticed the BMW trailing him? No, but it must be the same gray car that had nearly rear-ended his SUV as he was entering the hotel's parking lot. Obviously, someone was keeping an eye on him. The agent's shadow would know Trevor suspected something if he stopped now to examine the SUV. He'd have to find an opportunity to either ditch the transmitter or rent a car.

Should I shake my tail before meeting Lyn? He might report back to DNAY and catch up with me there anyway. Besides, he knows where I'm staying and most likely even what room is mine. Trevor decided to let the BMW follow him the short distance to DNAY. From there he'd try to get Lyn to drive her car and lose the tail — even if it would only be for the evening.

Andre watched Trevor step inside the SUV. When the vehicle rocked as the engine came to life, Andre started his Beemer. He expected the Highlander to pull out immediately, but the man seemed to be changing his clothes or something. Andre observed the vehicle closely in his mirror but didn't have a clear view of the SUV's cabin.

What the hell's he doing back there? The SUV began to move at last. Andre expected Trevor to turn to his right since the parking lot's exit was much closer if he went that way. Instead, the agent turned left. Andre looked to see if he could figure out what Trevor had been doing in his truck. The Fed was staring right at him. *Shit!* Andre jerked his head toward the hotel entrance. *Damn, that had to be as obvious as tits on a porn star.* Now he'd have to wait instead of driving after him straight away.

* * * *

Traffic was light. Trevor didn't stop to inspect his Toyota for unwanted surveillance equipment, and he arrived at the DNAY building in time to meet his date as she walked out the front door. "Lyn, you look fantastic!"

Her stunning smile widened, "Trevor, it's the same outfit I was wearing earlier today."

"I know, but you still look terrific." Trevor didn't see the BMW, but he wanted to leave quickly and to take Lyn's car to make it more difficult for them to be followed. "I'm not very familiar with Harrisburg. Is *La Cuisine* hard to find from here?"

"Tell you what," she grabbed his arm. "You may not have noticed, but I don't like to waste a lot of time." She leaned in and kissed him briefly. "I'll drive. My car's right over here." She pointed to a Lexus SC430 and hit the button on her keychain that unlocked the red convertible.

"Smells new. How long have you had her?"

"Just bought it about a month ago. Listen to this." She started the engine, backed out of the parking space, and drove through the parking lot to the stop sign at the road.

"It's quiet. What does it sound like when you're really moving?"

Although it was cool and windy, she pressed the button to lower the roof. Lyn peeled out onto the unlined two-lane roadway. The engine alternated between an aggressive roar and a loud purr as she shifted gears. "This car is the best toy I've bought for myself lately." She spoke loudly to be heard over the wind.

"I'd have thought you'd have plenty of men willing to get you any toys you wanted."

"Don't think," she instructed. She pushed another button and a classic pop channel played on the radio. Prince's "Little Red Corvette" blared out of the sound system. Trevor heard the lyric, "Baby, you're much too fast. You need a love that's gonna last." Was it fate or perhaps some sort of omen?

Making conversation he shouted over the music, "Is this a six cylinder?"

She shook her head and smiled that amazing smile again. "Eight. I don't want anything that's too small for my needs." Trevor saw her gaze move down past his abdomen. Lyn returned her attention to the road. Trevor wasn't sure because of the wind and the loud music, but he thought she'd said, "You should be just fine."

Andre found the unoccupied Highlander in the DNAY parking lot. He parked the BMW in a far corner of the lot, hoping the dark car wouldn't be apparent if the Fed returned to his SUV. Andre phoned the front desk. It was getting late, but Anthony answered the call. "Hey, it's Andre. Is that government agent, Trevor Byrne, in the building?"

"No. I think I saw him meet Ms. Flynn outside when she left about five minutes ago."

"Thanks." He ended the call and held a deep breath. Andre Slaughter was many things, but he was not a coward. He called Mr. Joseph. "It's Andre. I've lost him. His SUV is in the DNAY lot, but there's no sign of him. I believe he may have gone somewhere with your assistant. What would you like me to do, sir?"

The frosty voice was not menacing, only unemotional. "Thank you for your honesty, Mr. Slaughter. Yes, he did meet Ms. Flynn. I will receive her report tomorrow. Be available for my call any time after nine o'clock in the morning. I will update your instructions when we speak."

"Yes, sir. Thank you, sir." Andre's reply was not heard because his employer had already terminated the phone call.

The Lexus convertible's top was still closing as Trevor exited the car. He walked around to the front of the Lexus in time to see the valet blush when he glanced down at Lyn's chest. Trevor hoped he'd be so distracted that he'd forget to rummage through the car for cash or other valuables that Lyn might have left behind.

Between the somewhat expensive sports car and the fine restaurant Lyn had chosen, Trevor speculated that Lyn might be materialistic. She walked past him as he held the door. She was stunning and her hips swayed with the promise of raw, animal sex.

Trevor casually searched for a sign of the BMW that had followed him earlier. Seeing no indication of his tail, he entered the restaurant. He was impressed with the ebony wood and the apparently European paintings. Classical music played in the background to obscure the hushed conversations of the other couples. The ambiance was certainly an improvement over the movie posters and multiple television screens in the sports bars he frequented at home.

"*Bon soir, Madame.*"

"*Bon soir, Monsieur.* I have a reservation for two for Ms. Flynn," she responded in fluent French.

"Ah! Certainly, Ms. Flynn. This way please." The host answered her in French and motioned for the couple to follow. He led them upstairs to a secluded balcony table.

Lyn offered her, "*Merci,*" as the host seated her.

Trevor's French was rusty from disuse, but as he shook hands with the host, he slipped him a twenty and tried, "*Excellent! Merci beaucoup!*"

The gentleman bowed and wished them, "*Bon appétit.*"

The *garçon* immediately arrived with their menus and mentioned some of the house specialties. Lyn nodded occasionally, and Trevor caught bits and pieces. When the *garçon* left them alone on the upper level, Trevor commented, "Beautiful restaurant. The balcony is great—there's no one else up here." He glanced at the menu. "Do you know what you want?"

"Most of the time." Then the smile again—part gorgeous angel but with a hint of devil. She continued, "They make an unbelievable orange roughy here. I highly recommend it, especially with white burgundy."

The sommelier greeted them and offered a wine

menu. Trevor held up his hand to stop him. "*Pardon-moi, je parle un petit peu de français seulement.*" Although it was slow, the pronunciation was fairly accurate. Even if he had botched the statement, the sommelier would have understood that Trevor didn't speak much French. "*Une bouteille de burgundy blanc.*" He looked over to Lyn, "How do you say 'the best?'"

"You don't have to..."

"I know I don't have to, but I want to."

The sommelier cut in, "*Monsieur*, I do speak English as well. Do you know what meals you will be having this evening?" Trevor told him they were both having the orange roughy. "Sir, in my cellar, I have the perfect white burgundy to complement your choice." Trevor thanked him as he hurried away.

In a scolding but playful voice, Lyn asked, "Trevor Byrne, why did you just do that?"

He answered honestly, "You are the most amazing woman I've met. I want this evening to be perfect."

"I thought you were trying to impress me?"

"I figured I already did or you wouldn't be here with me this evening, especially since you had to change your plans."

The *garçon* returned and Lyn ordered. Trevor was relieved. He remembered that *poisson* was the French word for fish, but he wouldn't have gotten much farther than that. Fortunately, most of the missions he was assigned kept him within the United States, so his foreign language skills weren't usually critical.

Lyn turned the conversation to work. "So, Trevor,

how did I get lucky enough to meet you? What brought you to DNAY?"

He considered how much she might have been told by her employer. What, if anything, did she really know about the goings on at DNAY? He'd be cautious. "Routine business," he replied in way of a non-answer.

"Does your routine business often bring you to central Pennsylvania?"

"It takes me all over the country. I've been in Harrisburg and Lancaster before but not recently." The reply was sufficiently vague that it would not lead into a discussion of his last assignment in Pennsylvania.

"So what has you interested in DNAY?"

"A red flag went up when the Food and Drug Administration approved DNAY to test their treatment on people as quickly as they did. What do you know about the human testing phase you're about to start?"

"For the HIV-AIDS cure?" she asked innocently. He nodded. "I don't understand the science behind what we're doing, but we're on the cusp of finding a cure. We didn't want to wait years to finally try it out on humans. If it works on them like it has on the lab animals, we could eradicate the virus even if the person has already developed AIDS. We could change the lives of tens of millions of people. Why should the ones who are infected now have to suffer if we can do something about it?"

"Beneficial drugs have been presented to the FDA

many times before. Pharmaceutical companies with lots of money and political clout still had to wait until they could satisfy the people in charge. What makes this occasion so different?" Trevor inquired.

Lyn leaned forward and spread her hands apart expansively as she answered. "Trevor, think of the consequences. This is huge! If we can find a way to cure this epidemic, not only will those infected benefit, but so will society. Nobody will need to fear getting AIDS from sex or a blood transfusion. The current political administration will become heroes for pushing this through to make it available so quickly. We'll be rich. Everyone wins."

Trevor considered Lyn's justification. The Executive Branch of the government could apply immense pressure on one of its agencies if it anticipated a successful test. Any administration that saved millions of lives would easily win at least one more presidential election.

On the other hand, what if things weren't kosher? What if unsuspecting citizens lined up for this experiment, and it didn't work, or it somehow made them worse? If the results were terrible enough, would it come out that the President had pulled strings, and the public was harmed? Perhaps the real reason Trevor got this case was to be the President's insurance policy? Pull the plug on DNAY if this thing starts going down the toilet?

The agent chuckled. What the hell did it matter if he was being used as a political pawn? If he was potentially saving lives, he was being utilized much more effectively than if he was just handling administrative duties.

Lyn looked at him, but he only shrugged. She asked, "If you're so concerned, why don't you talk to someone at Food and Drug?"

"I tried that first." He watched Lyn for a reaction. Although there was no one within hearing range of the couple, Trevor kept his voice down. "The information provided to the FDA wasn't complete. They were unable to make a full evaluation before they approved the upcoming testing. It's unprecedented."

Lyn was puzzled. "That can't be right. The FDA would never approve this level of testing without enough data." She stared directly into his brown eyes, "Are you sure?" Everything about Lyn's body language led Trevor to believe this was news to her, or was she just a great actress?

Trevor nodded and switched back to his normal, baritone voice, "That's why I wanted to get a firsthand look at the facility and Mr. Joseph. See what kind of impression I'd get in person."

"What did you discover?"

"Two things. First, Karl Joseph is a hell of a sharp dresser. And second, something completely unexpected." Lyn tilted her head in surprise. "You." He grinned.

Whatever she was about to say was forgotten as the burgundy was presented to Trevor. He noted it came from a well-respected vineyard. He trusted that the sommelier had chosen a good year. "You certainly have my approval so far."

The man opened the bottle and offered the cork to Trevor. He glanced at it and nodded. The man poured a small portion into Trevor's glass. Trevor swirled it and breathed deeply. He tasted the wine and approved it with an enthusiastic, "It's perfect!"

The sommelier was pleased. He filled first Lyn's glass then Trevor's. He continued speaking to his customer in English, "If you need a second bottle, I do have another in my cellar."

Trevor handed this man a twenty also and dismissed him with a, "*Merci*." Trevor lifted his glass. "To an incredible woman."

"To a very special agent," she said and clinked her glass against his. A clear note sounded from the crystal. Trevor was extremely pleased with the wine. It should complement the fish quite well, but he would have to be careful not to drink too much. Wine and other alcohol made from grapes always hit him harder than either the Chivas scotch or the Smirnoff vodka he would normally select when drinking.

Since Lyn either did not know anything else about the HIV treatment—or at least wasn't volunteering information—Trevor took the opportunity to ask about her personal life. "So far we've talked about me and my job. I'd like to learn more about you. What do you like doing when you're not at work?"

"I have a small gym at home. I use it enough to keep myself toned. When I was younger, I did gymnastics, but now I just watch. I love ice skating!"

She lit up. He was lost in her emerald eyes.

The small talk continued over the best dinner of Trevor's life. They were drinking their after-dinner coffee when three armed men rushed into the restaurant.

All three wore blue jeans and gray ski masks. The first man to enter the restaurant was wearing a bulky knit sweater. From the balcony it was hard to tell, but the stripes seemed to be blue and tan. The man's arms were thick, but his stomach bulged against the sweater. Trevor suspected he had tried weight training for a few years then had given it up. The muscle had turned to fat. "Nobody move! This is a holdup!" the ex-weightlifter shouted. Trevor noticed a New Jersey accent. The robber ran to the kitchen to gather the employees into the main area. Whoever the robbers were, they were smart enough to keep an eye on everybody.

Trevor reached under the table and pressed the button to silence his phone. As slowly and quietly as possible, he removed the cell phone from his belt clip. Keeping it out of sight under the tablecloth, he thumbed it open with one hand. Without looking, he held the number one button in for several seconds. He placed the phone in the side pocket of his jacket away from the restaurant floor. Even though the thieves knew to bring everyone together, they must not have been familiar with the establishment because they didn't notice the balcony level and the couple dining there.

The second man wore a black mock turtleneck

that fit his form better than it matched his jeans. He was trim and spry, and the turtleneck accentuated his torso and powerful arms. He opened a large canvas duffel bag and ordered, "Put your wallets, watches, and jewelry in the bag! No sudden moves but make it fast!" Trevor heard a Jersey accent when the trim man spoke also. They weren't originally from this area and must not have realized there was an upper level to the restaurant. They had correctly determined the clientele were financially well-off. The nimble man started near the kitchen and worked his way forward.

Because of the distance and the angle, Trevor did not have a good view of the third man. The agent could see part of the man's ski mask but was aware that from where the criminal stood just inside the door, he could cover most of the patrons, especially those near the front of the restaurant.

Lyn whispered, "Do something!"

Trevor kept his nerves calm and his voice low. "They only want valuables, or they would have shot someone by now. They aren't from around here, so no one should recognize them. If they get what they want, no one will be hurt."

She shot a look down at the first level. "They don't even know we're up here. Couldn't you shoot one or two of them before they figure out what's happening?"

Trevor knew it would be dangerous to attempt anything with all the innocent diners and employees below. "I don't think anyone's in danger at the moment. It isn't worth risking anyone's life over money and jewelry."

After taking the cash from the register, the three thieves exited without firing a shot. They either didn't see the balcony or didn't want to take the time to work it.

Lyn asked, "Aren't you going to go after them?"

He pulled the cell phone out of his right-hand jacket pocket and laid it on the table. The timer continued to count how long the call had been in process. "The number one is programmed to speed dial nine-one-one. It also transmits GPS coordinates. The police should have had enough time to respond. I don't think those guys will get far."

Trevor pushed the button to return the phone to normal mode as he picked it up. The dispatcher was asking, "Hello, is anyone there? Please state the reason for your call. Hello?"

Trevor replied, "Three armed robbers just left *La Cuisine*. Have police arrived outside the restaurant yet?"

"No, sir. Until now nobody responded when I asked who was calling and why. I don't dispatch without a good reason. Who's calling?"

Trevor shook his head in disgust and flipped the phone shut, ending the call. The host rushed to their table. His French forgotten he asked, "Are you both okay?"

The agent looked over at his date before answering. "Yes, thank you. We're fine. The guests below may be more upset than we are." He flashed his badge too quickly for the host to get any information from it, especially in the dim light. "We need to leave immediately. Could you have someone bring us our check?"

Trevor paid the bill and handed a generous tip to the *garçon*. They followed him to the rear exit, avoiding eye contact with the other patrons. They stepped into the alleyway, and Lyn remarked, "I thought I'd get to see you in action back there." She sounded disappointed, but then her usual upbeat personality reasserted itself. "Maybe you were right. No one was hurt."

The valet parked Lyn's Lexus in front of the couple. Trevor tipped the valet and visually inspected his surroundings.

Lyn asked, "You don't think those guys are still around here do you?"

He had been searching for the gray BMW but didn't want to alarm her. Rather than tell her an outright lie, he replied, "No. I just wanted to make sure the coast was clear for our departure. No police in sight." No sign of the BMW either. Maybe they would be able to enjoy the rest of their evening. "Well, after that bit of excitement, where would you like to go?" He held her door opened while she got into the car then went around and let himself in.

"We could go back to my place and relax or watch a movie or something. I'll take you to work when I go in tomorrow and you can pick up your car."

"You have to work on Thanksgiving?"

"The world of science only stops for weekends, not for turkey. Well?"

"Your place sounds wonderful."

Lyn sped off into the night. She crossed the Susquehanna River to head toward her home in Camp Hill, on what she called "The West Shore." He gazed across the river at the nighttime Harrisburg skyline and wondered what it would look like in a few days if Karl Joseph's plan wasn't stopped.

Lyn's home was an inviting cape cod. Instead of using either of the two garage bays, she parked in the driveway. They walked up the stairs, and she opened the front door. Trevor looked around the living room as she turned the dimmer to bring the lights up halfway.

A large cream-colored leather sofa sat on one side of the room, across from the high definition plasma receiver. She led him to the couch. "It's still too early for the news. What do you usually watch on Wednesdays?"

He answered, "I don't really watch much TV. Put on whatever you like." He picked the remote off of the coffee table and handed it to her.

They watched some mindless reality shows and talked until Lyn turned on *Fox News at Ten*. When she saw *La Cuisine*'s façade on the screen, she turned up the volume.

The restaurant's host was being interviewed by a local reporter. *"Mon Dieu!* It was horrible. Three gunmen rushed in and stole everyone's valuables.

Then, they took the cash from our register. It was all so frightening. I feared someone would be hurt."

The reporter identified herself and her location, and the scene cut back to the news anchors at the studio desk. "At this time the armed robbers are still at large. Anyone with information, please call—" Lyn turned off the television.

"I can't believe they got away, Trevor. Excuse me a moment," Lyn left him alone. He wasn't sure if it was because seeing the event on the news shook her or if she wanted to freshen up.

Trevor stood and called after her, "I wouldn't have let anything happen to you."

He heard her, "I know," come from another room. It was followed by the crisp opening notes of a Sade song at a soothing volume from Bose speakers that Trevor noticed at each corner of the room. Recognizing the song, he correctly guessed that Lyn was playing Sade's greatest hits CD.

He turned to take a look at the painting he had glimpsed as he sat down with Lyn. On the wall, centered above the sofa, was a painting of a castle overlooking a lush green field, probably somewhere in Europe. Considering Lyn's long red hair, he decided it was in Ireland although it reminded him of similarly styled castles he's seen in Scotland.

His date walked behind him and wrapped her arms around his waist. She had sprayed on a light, flowery perfume. "Beautiful isn't it? It's the Macroom Castle. Built by the O'Floinns. If you go back several generations, my family lived there."

Trevor leaned closer to the painting, pulling her forward. "I don't see any mushrooms. Are you sure it's the Mushroom Castle?"

She slapped him playfully on the back. "Macroom," she said slowly. "Macroom Castle."

Both to remember the name and to show Lyn that he had heard it properly, he repeated, "Macroom Castle. Now I've got it!"

Trevor turned to face Lyn without breaking the embrace. His eyes locked onto hers. In the modest light, her pupils were large ebony pools in a sea of emerald. He gasped and realized she'd literally taken his breath away. "Have you ever been there?"

She whispered into his ear. "My parents took me when I was a wee lass. It was in ruins because of a fire. I've seen photos of me at the remains, but I don't remember being there."

"That's a shame. It must have been quite impressive in its time."

"Nothing lasts forever, Trevor. That's why I enjoy life every day. You know, I'd love to see the castle again. Would you take me...all the way?" She moved his hands down to her rear and pushed her pelvis forward.

Trevor kissed her. His heart beat faster, and his breathing became shallow. He opened his eyes to make sure Lyn's were closed. His tongue entered her mouth, and she began to remove her clothes.

She slipped her jacket off, and Trevor removed his own. Lyn loosened his tie and pulled it over his head. He did the same with her chemise. He was spellbound by her barely covered, voluptuous breasts. The full, round orbs strained to free themselves from her white lace bra. Lyn moaned in response to the bulge in Trevor's pants.

Lyn unbuttoned his shirt. Trevor slid the bra's straps off her arms and brushed the cups down. She began to squirm, and he found that her skirt and panties were gone. Lyn finished undressing him then led him to the sofa and pushed him down on his back. The song playing now was his favorite Sade song, the improved version of "Never as Good as the First Time."

Trevor lost track of the music when Lyn straddled him. Their bodies fit together perfectly. He had no idea how long he had been swimming in a sea of sensations, but when he opened his eyes again, they were both sweating. He listened to her squeals of pleasure as she built up through a series of progressively more powerful orgasms while he enjoyed the beauty of her glistening skin as she rocked and her breasts bounced. He sat up and smelled her. Tasted her. Lyn's intensity overwhelmed him. He lay back and grabbed her hips. He pulled her against him with his remaining strength and thrust. Lyn's legs quivered. She screamed, and Trevor felt her nails scratching trails along his biceps. He climaxed deep inside her.

Lyn leaned forward and nuzzled the side of his face. She stretched on top of him and moaned in his ear, "Mmmm, Trevor."

"You're incredible, Lyn." Her thigh rubbed along

his, and she nibbled his ear.

Lyn's green eyes sparkled when she chuckled and huskily replied, "I know."

For the first hour or so, Trevor slept well. Then, his dreams turned to nonsensical nightmares. The last one he could recall in the morning involved a giant black widow spider. It was smiling as it approached to bite off his head. The rest of the night he tossed and turned but couldn't fall into a deep sleep.

He showered and dressed in the same clothes he had worn last night, sans the tie. He went to the kitchen. Lyn wore a business suit similar to the one she had worn yesterday, only this one was a heavier wool, in a midnight blue herringbone pattern. Again, her short skirt and shoes matched. She was taking two plates of French toast and sausage links into her dining room. "You're even more beautiful than yesterday," Trevor complimented her. He grabbed the orange juice and followed.

They went back to collect the coffee, butter, and maple syrup. "Thanks."

Trevor downed two glasses of orange juice with his breakfast. "That was great. Do you always eat this well in the morning?"

Lyn smiled, still basking in the afterglow of their lovemaking. "Only when I've worked up an appetite the night before."

They made small talk as she drove him from her Camp Hill home to the DNAY lab. Traffic was light because of the holiday. The sky was a crisp blue with only occasional clouds speeding to some unknown destination.

Lyn had a carefree playfulness that Trevor found alluring. He asked, "Last night was wonderful. Can I see you again? Soon?"

"Meet me at my house at four Saturday afternoon."

"Terrific. Let me get your home address and phone number to make sure I can find you." He took her business card from his wallet and wrote the information she provided on the back. She parked in her assigned space, and Trevor got out of the Lexus. "I'm looking forward to seeing you Saturday."

Lyn slung her purse over her shoulder and locked the doors with her keychain remote. "Me, too. Don't be late."

"I'll be on time." He promised. He watched as she walked from her convertible to the sliding glass doors. Her legs moved her quickly and surely across the short distance. They were not quivering the way they had last night. Her backside swayed under her tight blue skirt.

Lyn stopped before going inside. She turned to look in his direction. When she saw he was still watching her, she smiled brightly and waved. Trevor already had a lifetime full of memories—some good, some horrible. However, he knew then and there that Lyn's dazzling image at the entranceway to DNAY was burned forever into his memory. No matter how long their relationship lasted—even if he only saw her once more—he'd never forget the way the morning sun highlighted her red hair and glinted off her jade eyes as she smiled and waved to him. He returned the smile and wave, feeling like an ecstatic schoolboy.

Lyn turned away and entered the building. Trevor stood in the parking lot and deeply breathed in the cool air. A car pulled into the lot, an employee arriving for his shift. The spell was broken. Lyn was gone, the entranceway empty. He exhaled and slowly walked to his Highlander.

While walking to his SUV, Trevor scanned the parking lot for the dark gray sports car that had been following him. He didn't see the vehicle, but rather than take any chances, he got in the Highlander and drove through the lot without searching for the tracking device he knew must be somewhere near the rear of his Toyota.

He called his case manager. "Happy Thanksgiving, Earl. Trevor here."

"What did you find out?"

"I don't think Lyn knows anything, but she might have just been covering for her boss. I'm not sure. She might have even been trying to get information from me."

"Keep me posted."

"I need you to run a plate for me. A dark gray BMW 525 has been following me. It has Pennsylvania tag B B E three oh three five." He heard Earl jotting a note on a pad before he keyed the information into his computer. Trevor knew Earl would soon have the intel on the BMW's owner. "By the way, how is Doctor Singh's family?"

"As of this morning, they were fine. No one tried anything. Ah, here we go. The car tailing you is registered to Andre Slaughter. He looks like a thug on his license photo. Let's see if he has any priors." The sound of the keyboard clicking carried through the phone connection. "And speaking of thugs, we still haven't had any luck with that man who broke into your home. From what you told me about him, you might want to consider moving."

"Might not be a bad idea. I'll think about it."

"Okay. Andre Slaughter. One arrest, tried for homicide, acquitted. Doesn't seem like he should have been able to afford the attorney he used based on the income he reported to the IRS. Let me give you the address and phone numbers I found for him. Maybe they'll be useful." He provided the information to his agent.

"Earl, the HIV test is tomorrow. I don't have anything substantial, but I think we should have the FDA or someone pressure DNAY into postponing. They obtained FDA approval by coercion, they hired someone to break into my home and possibly kill me, I'm sure they killed Doctor Singh, and they are tailing a government agent. Something big is about to go down. I'm sure of it."

"No way I can get a postponement. There's too much political clout being thrown around. I didn't tell you yet about DNAY's majority stockholder."

Trevor's interest was piqued. "Who is it?"

"Mark Johns and Luke Matthews as co-trustees for the Fundamental Christian Believers Society."

"Are those names for real? It sounds like they were named after the gospels of the New Testament."

Earl chuckled. "Pretty obvious. Even though I'm an atheist, I picked up on that. I tried to use the agency database to find out more about the FCBS. A big yellow and black warning flag has been slapped on their files. They're off limits to us."

Trevor had to know more. "That restriction could only have been placed by someone above your level if you weren't able to access the information. Who classified it? Why?"

"I've been around here long enough to know you don't push buttons you're not supposed to push. When I got the warning, I stopped using the agency database to find out more about them."

"That doesn't give us too much more. Why would a fundamental Christian group invest heavily in a genetics research company? Aren't they usually opposed to gene research and cloning, playing God and all that?"

"Exactly what I wondered. So, I did some searching on the Internet. Mark Johns and Luke Matthews are listed as officers of the Fundamental Christian Believers Society. The rest of the officers all have combinations of Biblical names as well. An apostle's name combined with a name from someone in the Old Testament. A saint's name and a king's name. A statistician would have a brain aneurism trying to figure the odds of something like this occurring randomly."

"What are we going to do about it?"

"Stay away from the FCBS, Trevor. I have a number of other projects I could use your experience on right now, but the DNAY case stinks like a garbage heap. What would you need to get in there tonight? If further action is warranted against DNAY, I'll grant you full authorization to do what you deem necessary." Earl repeated, "Now, what do you need?"

A NEW ATTITUDE

Deanne was excited. Today her family would enjoy Thanksgiving dinner. Tomorrow she'd take a taxi downtown and get her treatment. Would the medicine or vaccine or whatever it was work? Would she be cured? She'd be sure to thank God in advance today when she prayed. She drank her instant coffee and scoured the classified ads with renewed interest.

She felt her luck was changing for the better. Deanne was blessed to live so close to this company's lab, so she could be part of the free testing phase. If it worked, people across the country would have to pay a fortune for the cure.

Today she'd already discovered four ads that looked promising. She'd circled them and would type cover letters and résumés before the big meal. If these didn't pan out, there would be other, better opportunities. She'd find something that paid well enough that she could move out of her parents' house before she destroyed their marriage. *Watch out world: Deanne Baker is back!*

Trevor decided to go out for lunch a little after noon. He saw a Thanksgiving buffet advertised on an outdoor sign at the diner just down the boulevard from his hotel. He pulled into the parking lot and got out of the SUV. He went around to the back of the vehicle and took a quick look around the small parking lot. He hadn't seen the BMW so far. Perhaps Andre was letting the leash out. He doubted that his observer had been called off.

He knelt near the rear bumper. He ran his hand underneath and felt nothing unusual. He bent down farther and looked at the underside of his SUV. "There you are you little son of a bitch." It was well out of sight, but Trevor had located the GPS transmitter that was attached to his vehicle's chassis.

He was about to pull it off but then reconsidered. *No. Let the bastard find me. If he does, I'll be ready for him.*

He pressed the button on his keychain to lock the SUV, walked up the stairs, and entered the diner. He realized it didn't offer the best defensive options. In addition to the diner he'd entered, there was another section to his right. He could sit at one of the open booths to his left, which would provide a view of anyone entering through either doorway. However, the buffet sounded good, and he didn't want to be stuck in a booth ordering a menu meal.

He walked into the other section and saw that this side was a sports bar. The buffet was set up along the far wall, a little to his right. The tables were occupied, but he saw one in the corner, just past the buffet, that seemed empty.

Trevor scanned the faces of the patrons as he walked across the bar. It was a diverse crowd although the majority were white. Their ages ranged from seniors to children. Mostly couples, but some larger groups too, probably friends who decided to get together or families who couldn't convince one of their own to prepare the meal.

He didn't see the man who'd been following him. He reached the table and sat in the corner of the room. He moved the chair, so he could better see the people at the buffet and the door to his left. When no one was at the buffet, he could even see customers entering from the door on this side. *Best seat in the house*, he thought.

He'd only been seated for a few minutes when the busy waitress had an opportunity to approach his table. "Haven't seen you here before. New to the area?"

"I only expect to be here a few days. Do you get a regular crowd here?"

"Some of them come here a lot. Then, we get the construction workers in town for a few months. I know I'd remember if I saw you before."

She was busy, but she still had the time to be cute and sexy too. He smiled at her. "I'll just have the buffet and some coffee." He saw the various sweeteners on the table but no creamer. "And cream."

She smiled back, "You sure that's all you want?"

He nodded. "At least for right now."

She left to get the coffee, and he walked over to the buffet. He stood in line behind two young guys. "Thanks for dinner, Mo." The one speaking looked around anxiously. "This was a good idea, but I didn't think it would be this crowded on a holiday." He loaded his plate like it was the first meal he'd eaten in weeks. Trevor hoped there would still be food left on the buffet for him.

"At least it's not packed full on our side. Anyway, since my parents were away this year, I'm glad you could come out with me, Ray. Happy Thanksgiving, man." The two walked away to the diner side.

Trevor piled his plate with turkey, mashed potatoes, and stuffing. He smothered it all with the thick turkey gravy, added some cranberry sauce and sweet potatoes, and returned to his table. The coffee and cream were already there.

Before digging in, he silently prayed. *God, thank you for all of your blessings and this meal. Please forgive my sins and help me to successfully complete this mission. Amen.*

He enjoyed the meal but only had seconds of the coffee. He looked at his check and saw the waitress' name and phone number were written on it with a big smiley face and a question mark. He tore off the part of the check with her information and folded it into his wallet for possible future use. He left enough cash to cover the bill and a substantial tip.

He walked out the closest door, looked around, and, instead of walking directly to his Highlander, walked around to the back of the building. No sign of the dark gray BMW. He turned and walked to his SUV.

He had some time to kill, so he decided to call Harvey Franks at Three Mile Island. It took him a minute to get connected. "Harv. It's Trevor Byrne. How's your Thanksgiving going?"

"Quiet, except for the extra guardsmen parading around inside my facility. Have you learned anything else?"

"Nothing concrete. I'm sure something is about to happen, but I still don't know what."

"Let me know either way when you do." Franks ended the call.

Trevor drove out of the parking lot wondering how Lyn's day was going.

INTERROGATION

The cold voice on her intercom ordered, "Ms. Flynn, my office. Now." She knew it was time to make her report on the evening she'd spent with Trevor. *What would he ask? What will I tell?* If everything at DNAY was legitimate, would her employer be so determined to learn more about a federal agent? It didn't make sense.

She took her time walking over to the CEO's office. The door was open. She pocketed her passkey since she wouldn't need it to enter his office this time. She closed her eyes and took a deep breath.

"Have a seat, Ms. Flynn." Karl Joseph closed the door behind her. "Now, tell me everything about your evening with Agent Byrne."

"We went out to dinner at *La Cuisine.* He ordered an expensive bottle of white burgundy, and we both had the orange roughy."

Karl mentally noted that the agent drank as he returned to his desk. Perhaps he could slip something into a glass of the agent's wine if the opportunity arose. He motioned for his executive secretary to continue.

"We were having a good time, and then three armed robbers burst into the restaurant and stole money and jewelry from the patrons and staff."

Karl's eyes widened with interest. "What did he do? Tell me exactly."

The woman trembled slightly, but thank God she seemed to collect herself quickly. "We were seated upstairs in the balcony section. It was dimmer there than on the main floor because we didn't have a chandelier hanging down over our table, and the stairs are hard to see from the main dining area. They didn't spot us. I expected Trevor to try to stop them, but he just sat there."

Karl tilted his head in surprise. "He did nothing at all?"

The woman shook her head then seemed to change her mind. "Well, he had dialed nine-one-one from his cell phone. He thought with the GPS tracking that the police would be waiting outside to capture the robbers. Unfortunately, the call was received by an idiot who didn't dispatch any officers. When we watched the news last night, the crooks were still at large. I guess the thieves got away."

Karl leaned back. The agent didn't take direct action but did attempt to defeat the criminals. Subtly. Karl would take this threat seriously. Agent Byrne must die. There was too much at stake to underestimate this detective. Mr. Slaughter had handled matters for Karl's associates on more than one occasion in the past and came with strong references, but had he ever gone against an opponent like Agent Byrne was shaping up to be? "Go on..."

She continued, "We left the restaurant before the

police arrived. Then, we went back to my place."

Karl quickly realized the possible significance of this piece of information. *The agent didn't wait around and make a statement. That would certainly have been protocol. He either plays by his own rules or, perhaps, is above routine law?*

"Anyway, that's about it," she sat back and crossed her arms over her disgustingly large bosom.

"I don't believe that is everything, Ms. Flynn. I must know more. First, what does he know or suspect about DNAY? Why was he here?"

She fidgeted, typical woman gathering her thoughts and trying to express her feelings in words. Karl drummed his fingers on his desk until she began. "I'm not exactly sure why, but he seems concerned that the FDA approval we received for the testing tomorrow was approved so rapidly. He asked me about it. I told him both DNAY and the FDA feel the potential for success is too great to wait. Too many lives could be ruined or lost in the interim."

Karl replied, "Precisely, Ms. Flynn. Now the other item we must discuss." Karl paused. "Did you and he have sex?"

Lyn's head shot up. She felt herself blush. This inquisition had gone too far. "Mr. Joseph! That's none of your business."

The bastard was sitting there calm and unemotional. "Yes, Ms. Flynn, it is my business. I run this company. You are my executive secretary. If you cannot assist me properly, you will be replaced. I would like your help to determine if there is a peril to the company." Oh he was a cold, heartless bastard.

"I don't understand how telling you about my sex life can help the corporation."

"Perhaps if I tell you what specific information I am seeking, it will be less embarrassing for you. Agent Byrne may be a clever and resourceful opponent. What you will tell me, Ms. Flynn, is your assessment of his physical strength and stamina. Am I clear?"

She rubbed her head. It felt as though she was getting a migraine. She'd begin looking for another job next week, and she'd call Trevor. He was right— something was happening here. She had no more doubts. "I was quite pleased with his strength and stamina." Karl turned white and seemed to sink into his seat. Lyn thought he wanted to vomit. Could she learn anything from this meeting that would be useful to Trevor? Now was probably her best chance to get answers. "If we're not doing anything wrong, why would he be a danger to you?"

The color returned to Karl's face at this challenge. "Ms. Flynn, tomorrow we undertake the largest experiment this civilization has ever known. If all goes as planned, we will change the world. I won't let anything stop that. Tomorrow will be a long day. Don't make any plans for the evening. That will be all for now, Ms. Flynn."

He had what he wanted from her, and now she was dismissed. Typical man. No, men were cold, but cold was just the tip of the iceberg for this bastard.

* * * *

Karl had dismissed Ms. Flynn already, why was she still sitting there? Finally, the bitch straightened her back, stood, and muttered, "Yes, sir." Karl watched disinterestedly as she opened the door and walked out of his office. He got up, closed the door, returned to his desk, and picked up his phone.

He heard the cell phone over Kei's passionate screams. He knew from the ringtone that he couldn't ignore this call, no matter how badly timed. He was hot and sweaty and tried to control his breathing before he answered the urgent call. "Andre here."

The voice on the other end of the call was even more chilling than usual. Andre felt the cold run through him and knew this session with Kei was over. "Mr. Slaughter. I have determined that our problem must be eliminated as soon as practical. Make it clean and quiet. We don't want to disturb anyone."

Andre was not surprised by the new instructions. "Yes, sir. Consider it done."

His employer added, "Don't disappoint me this time. I haven't forgotten your last failure. Notify me when you've completed your assignment. Am I clear?"

"He won't bother you again, sir."

The call was finished and so was he. He'd take care of the agent at his hotel. Maybe he'd even get back in time to give Kei another reason to be thankful tonight.

* * * *

As soon as Lyn was out of her boss' sight, she hurried to her office and slammed the door. She threw her passkey on her desk and picked up the telephone. Thinking better of it, she hung up the office phone.

Her hands shook as she opened the bottom right desk drawer and removed the nearly full bottle of Absolut Raspberri vodka. She filled her empty coffee mug and downed half of the drink. Her hands still shaking, she refilled the mug and stashed the bottle in its usual place behind her files. She'd never felt so not in control. She took another long drink and tried to fight back the tears as she logged in to her computer. She opened her résumé but couldn't focus on the document or her career.

She didn't know what her boss was really up to, but she knew if anyone could stop his plan, it was Trevor. How could she uncover DNAY's secret? For the first time, she realized how little information she could access from her computer terminal. What would she be looking for? Where could she find it? She rubbed her eyes to wipe away the tears and noticed the passkey on her desk. Of course. The most secure office in the building was Karl Joseph's, and Lyn was one of the few people with access.

She grabbed her cell phone, found Trevor's number, and dialed it. "Come on. Answer," she willed.

"Trevor."

Lyn cried as she told him about the inquiry and

how the meeting and Trevor's suspicions convinced her that something was wrong at DNAY. "I'm not sure when everyone will leave tonight. Hopefully, most of them will go home early for the holiday. I'm going to see if I can find out what's really going on here."

Trevor sounded stern. "Lyn, I'm infiltrating DNAY tonight. Get out of there. It's not safe. If you want to help, meet me and tell me about the layout: where's Karl's office? The labs?"

"Oh come on! I work here. Why wouldn't I be safe? I'm going to stay here tonight and pack a few personal items before I go. Once Mr. Joseph leaves, I'll look through his files. Maybe I'll discover something in his office or on his computer."

"Lyn, don't be stupid! It'll be dangerous. I'll do it. Just give me the codes and tell me where the offices and labs are located."

"You wouldn't be able to get into the building without Mr. Joseph being informed. If I get caught, it's not a big deal since I work here," she reasoned.

"Lyn, I'll do it alone. If I have to, I'll come over and drag you out for your own safety. Please. Get out. Right now."

Lyn laughed. "Big tough guy. You'd never get to my office. Security would stop you before you made it to the elevators."

"Lyn, I'm not joking. Get out. I'll look around tonight."

"Trevor, even if you somehow got inside the building without being caught, you'd never get into

Mr. Joseph's office without tripping the alarm. There's a digital data card reader, and he's also got an optical retina scanner."

"You could give me your pass, and I could take a high-definition digital close-up photo of your eyes. Printed out the right size on a state of the art printer it should fool his scanner."

"Forget it. This system is one hundred percent secure. I'll get in, see what I can find, and leave."

"Leave now and don't go back. Not tonight, not ever." Trevor tried again. *Damn, he's stubborn.* She was too independent to be swayed. "I want to know what's going on as much as you. I'm sure it's important. Mr. Joseph wouldn't be so concerned about you if it wasn't." Her words poured out rapidly. She couldn't stop herself. "Trevor, I've spent my life playing the game. Getting ahead. Earning as much as possible, so I could have whatever I wanted. I've always done everything for myself. Everyone I've known has, but you're different. You don't put yourself first. You help others. I've been so shallow. I'm not going to be like that any more. I want to make a difference."

Silence. Then, "I understand what you're saying, Lyn, but I've had years of training and experience. I should be there to protect you."

"I'll be fine. How about this? If Mr. Joseph is still here or it looks like I can't get into his office without someone knowing, I'll just forget about it and leave around six. Whatever happens, I'll call you and tell you how I make out."

"I don't like it, Lyn. Call me right away if you change your mind."

"I'll talk to you soon. Bye."

UNEXPECTED VISITOR

Trevor had spent the afternoon driving around to become more familiar with the area. He finally returned to the Handi Hotel. Driving through the parking lot, he still saw no sign of Andre's BMW. He backed into a space near the main entrance and went into the hotel. Tiffany had already left the front desk. The woman working there was neither as young nor attractive as Tiffany. An elderly couple was checking in. The agent walked over and stopped behind the pair but close enough to hear what was being discussed.

Trevor could tell from the clerk's gruff voice that she was not nearly as friendly as the outgoing brunette who had checked him into the hotel. In a sharp tone, the clerk corrected the embarrassed man standing before the counter. "I said to fill in *this* section and sign *here*. You weren't supposed to do anything down *there*."

Color rose to the man's face, possibly for the first time in years by the look of his pale complexion. He apologized, making an excuse about his new bifocals.

Now that her power had been asserted, the clerk assured the travelers she would be able to fix this serious problem for them even though it wasn't normal procedure. She leisurely finished processing the transaction and handed them two keycards at last.

"Enjoy your stay at the Handi."

As the couple walked away, Trevor overheard the wife nag, "Harry, why do you let people treat you like that? You need to stick up for yourself! You should have told her..." and the one-sided discussion drifted out of hearing range.

Trevor approached the desk, introduced himself to the woman behind the counter, and asked if she had a package for him.

"Are you a guest?" she asked abruptly, rather than consult the computer in front of her.

Maintaining his patience, Trevor replied, "Yes. I have room 419."

"Give me your identification and room key." Trevor took his time retrieving the items she demanded. He placed them on the countertop and slid them toward her.

She picked up his Maryland driver's license and examined it closely. Then, she swiped the door key through a reader to confirm it was still active. Placing his license and the room key on the lower counter and leaving them there, out of Trevor's reach, she turned and shuffled over to inspect the cubbyholes behind her. She shambled back to the counter and said, "No package. Only a letter." She had not brought the envelope with her.

"May I have the letter, please, Dawn?" he asked, reading the name on her badge.

"You didn't ask about a letter."

"I didn't know I had one until you told me." He heard a sigh behind him and knew the next victim was already irritated by the reception desk clerk's personality.

Dawn retrieved the letter and slapped it down on the counter along with his license and room key. Her gray eyes seemed to challenge him with the stare of a disgruntled postal worker ready to reach for her assault rifle.

"Thank you, Dawn. Can someone notify me as soon as my delivery arrives?"

"Do you see anyone else here? No. That's because I'm the only one on duty." Trevor was about to speak, but she abruptly held up her hand the way a crossing guard would if stopping a car. "I'll call you, but only if I have the time."

"Good evening, Dawn." Trevor picked up the letter and moved to the unoccupied end of the counter.

Dawn was already reprimanding the woman who had walked up to her counter. "I didn't call you. You'll have to wait."

The unsealed Handi guest envelope was simply addressed 'Trevor.' The hastily printed message on the hotel's guest stationary read 'I'm waiting for you!'

Lyn kept herself busy at her desk until Mr. Joseph left the office that evening. She waited another half hour, so she wouldn't arouse any suspicion from the guards. This late on a holiday, only the security detail would still be in the facility.

She steeled herself and decided that it was now or never. The executive secretary randomly took some folders from her desk and put a very concerned look on her face. She walked purposefully to the CEO's office. Of course, he was gone, and his door was locked.

Lyn swiped her keycard in the slot and stared into the retinal scanner. The audible chirp and the accompanying green light signaled her authority to enter. The door swung open silently, and she closed it behind her.

Trevor folded the letter and shoved it into the back pocket of his jeans. He scanned the hotel lobby but saw no sign of Andre Slaughter or anything suspicious. Was it a warning that Andre was waiting in his room for him? Or that he was waiting and could take him out at any time, any place?

Rather than possibly trap himself in the confines of an elevator, Trevor took the fire stairs up to the fourth floor. He cautiously looked out the door's window. He saw no one and slowly opened the door. Leaning his head through the entranceway, he looked down the empty hallway. He entered the corridor and tuned his senses to listen for doors and footsteps or any other movement.

The elevator bell chimed, and Trevor flattened himself along the near wall. He unzipped his jacket, ready to reach for his SW99. A middle-aged man with graying hair and a tote bag bulging nearly as much as the man's gut exited the elevator. His gray pinstripe wool suit had seen better days, and the shoes were still serviceable but badly in need of a shine. The ensemble screamed less-than-successful salesman. If the man had been in better physical condition, Trevor might have suspected him as one of Andre's undercover associates packing a submachine gun in the tote. Without noticing the agent, the salesman rushed to his room, eager to spend the evening away from his family.

Nobody else came out of the elevator, but Trevor waited until the doors closed and the lift resumed its journey before he continued to his room. The radio inside was loudly playing some pop dance number that he'd heard before but couldn't name. Was it loud enough to cover the noise of a silenced firearm?

Trevor disliked sound suppressors because they had a tendency to catch in a holster when drawn. Carrying a silenced weapon could slow the draw enough to make the difference in a gunfight—the difference between life and death. If Andre was going to use one, it would be drawn before Trevor entered the room. Trevor held the room key in his left hand and pulled the pistol from his shoulder holster. If he needed to use the .45, the radio would not conceal its booming discharge.

He knelt to the side of the door and inserted the keycard. The green light glowed, and the lock noisily clicked open. No gunfire yet. He reached up and opened the door a crack. Still nothing. He slammed the door with his shoulder and rolled into the room, coming up on one knee. The gun's muzzle swept across the bed, stopping when the front sight was aimed at the nude woman, who had sat up and screamed. The blanket had fallen down and exposed her perky breasts and the small nipple rings she wore today.

"Tiffany?" Trevor asked. "What are you doing here?" He returned the gun to his holster, stood, and closed the door to his room.

She pointed at the package on the nearest nightstand. "When your package came priority from DSL, I wanted to make sure you got it. And I thought you might want to have some fun." She pulled the blanket the rest of the way down, exposing her shaved mound. "Didn't you get the note I left for you at the desk?"

Trevor smiled and relaxed. "It wasn't signed." He placed his jacket on a hanger and put the holsters and guns in the safe, so they wouldn't frighten Tiffany.

Tiffany came over to Trevor and pressed her naked body against him. The excitement evident in her voice, she asked, "What do you need those for? What do you do?"

He led her back to the bed and handed her the clothes scattered on the floor. "I work for the government. After getting an anonymous note and hearing my radio, I didn't want to take any chances."

"I don't either." Tiffany handed him a condom. She looked down at the bulge in Trevor's pants. "I didn't know to buy the large ones," she purred and dropped the pile of clothes back onto the worn carpet.

It had been much easier to say no to Tiffany's advances when she was wearing some clothing, no matter how revealing she managed to make it. She made his decision even more difficult when she sat on the bed and began rubbing one of her hands across her breasts and the other between her thighs. Her hazel eyes gazed at him with blatant yearning. Her skin shimmered with a light coat of sweat, and she was already on the brink of giving herself an orgasm. Trevor breathed in deeply and pulled a chair over beside the bed. He sat and watched Tiffany enjoy her own body. He took another breath and resolved not to touch the young hotel clerk.

"Tiffany, you must go." Trevor leaned to pick up her clothing once more.

Tiffany screamed out in ecstasy, and her sharp fingernails left thin, crimson trails across her breasts. Trevor started to sit up, holding Tiffany's outfit, when the door burst open and a stern voice ordered, "Sit up real slow, fucker."

Lyn looked around the office. It was unoccupied, as she'd expected. The workplace was free of clutter and unnecessary furnishings. Besides the desk, chairs, and credenza, there was only Mr. Joseph's coat tree, which held some freshly pressed dry cleaning. Her search shouldn't take long. The credenza was unlocked, and she carefully scanned the files. A thorough examination revealed nothing unusual. If there was anything to find in his office, it had to be in the computer.

As closely as she'd worked with her boss, she'd had many opportunities to observe him enter his password: *Zorn-des-Gottes*. Sometime she would have to run the phrase through a German-English translator to see what it meant. She typed it in and soon his personalized desktop displayed. The background image showed an open padlock superimposed upon a double helix, reflecting intense sunlight—the DNAY corporate logo floating in a blue sky. The slogan the ad agency had created was written in a golden font below the logo: "When the secret of DNA is unlocked, it will be mankind's brightest day."

Lyn opened Microsoft Word and clicked on "File" to see the listing of recently accessed Word documents. Eyeing the list, she found one titled "HIV Trials..." She double-clicked the link and saw that the full title of the document was "HIV Trials Final Report." If the human trials had not even started, how could a final report have been prepared?

Reading the document, she saw the report ended with the recently completed phase of animal testing and a prediction: "Vapor should prove instantly fatal to all mammals with any stage HIV infection. Not potent after twelfth day. Contents of tank A, if released into environment, are sufficient to circulate globally within potency period."

"Dear God! He's not trying to cure AIDS—he's trying to kill everyone with HIV!" Lyn was so intent on the report that she failed to notice the door open silently, and the muscular blond man enter with his handgun drawn.

"You're quite right, Ms. Flynn. Remain seated. There's one more thing I need you to do for me."

GLOBAL CLEANSING

Andre closed the door and repeated, "Sit up real slow and drop what you're holding."

Trevor was furious at himself for being caught unprepared — his guns locked in the safe behind his armed adversary. The agent nodded his head toward the pile of clothing that was yet again heaped on the floor. "Do you mind if she gets dressed?" Tiffany pulled the cover around her.

Andre leaned against the chest of drawers, keeping his gun trained on the man he'd been following. "Yeah, I do mind." Pointing the gun at Trevor for emphasis he said, "I want you to sit there with your hands in your lap. Her," pointing the gun at the brunette, "I want naked."

Tiffany pleaded, "Please, Mr. Holmes. I won't say anything, I promise. Let me leave."

"Let the girl go, Andre."

"I have plans for her, and they don't include letting her go." He swung the gun back at Trevor and aimed the muzzle at the agent's groin. "How do you know my name?"

"Because you're sloppy, Slaughter. Not like that other guy your boss sent to take care of me."

"Who're you talkin' about?"

"I don't know. A black guy, bigger than you.

Better than you, but I kicked his ass, and he ran away before I got any answers."

"Fuck you, man. When they want the best, they hire me. I'm gonna hit you like thunder, fucker."

"What? A lot of noise but nothing to fear?"

Andre stormed across the space separating him from Trevor. He pulled his gun hand back to pummel the agent.

Expecting the assault, Trevor reacted. While Andre was pulling his arm back, Trevor leapt out of the chair, grabbed Andre's wrist and slammed it back into the wall. The gun fell to the floor.

Trevor squeezed his other hand around Andre's neck and slammed his head against the wall. He noticed Tiffany running from the room with her clothes. While he was distracted, Andre brought his knee into Trevor's groin. The agent fell hard to his knees.

Andre kicked Trevor in the back, and the agent sprawled on the floor. He struggled to push himself up and his right hand brushed against Andre's fallen pistol. Andre kicked again. Trevor felt a rib break as he heard the crack. He groaned and, holding the gun, brought his arm back along his side. He rolled over, and Andre's next kick landed in his stomach. He groaned again and opened his watering eyes. He aimed the gun in Andre's direction and with a hoarse voice ordered, "Stop or I'll kill you."

Andre laughed. "You're in no shape to kill anyone. The gun's not even pointing at me." He kicked out, and the gun flew across the room. Using both hands, he pulled Trevor up by his shirt and slammed him into the wall.

Trevor's head bounced, and his broken rib hurt like hell. His back slid down the wall, and he sat on the floor gasping for breath.

Andre hovered near him, waiting to see if he'd rise and attempt another attack. Eventually he crossed the room, retrieved the gun, and returned to Trevor. "You play a good game, but this is checkmate."

His executive secretary jumped and let out a squeal when she heard his voice. Karl motioned with the muzzle of his pistol for her to sit. "Mr. Joseph, I..." she began.

"Ms. Flynn, do not insult my intelligence. Even if I had not heard your remark when you discovered my plan, there would be no reason for your presence in front of my computer. You have access to everything you need from the network."

She placed her hands in her lap and seemed to be studying them. "How can you do such a thing? I thought we were trying to save people—not kill them."

"Ms. Flynn, you do realize most males who have been infected by HIV are homosexuals?" She muttered a response that he neither heard nor cared to hear. "Homosexuals have been cursed by God. In the past, He has intervened to destroy large populations of them. Sodom and Gomorrah for instance. With modern technology, we have developed an airborne agent that I shall unleash to wipe this planet's filthy slate clean. I shall save Him the trouble of becoming personally involved this time. Do you see?" She shook her head and began to tremble. *Pathetic.*

"I can obliterate most of the male homosexual population, as well as their female lovers who are no longer clean. As a bonus, I will eliminate a vast number of drug addicts. Society will be cleansed! I will be God's instrument on Earth!"

RUNNING OUT OF TIME

Trevor saw the policemen rush into his room, sidearms drawn. "Police! Drop the weapon and put your hands in the air!"

Andre spun toward the cops in surprise. Trevor lunged at Andre and tackled him. One officer's heel ground Andre's wrist against the floor. Andre grimaced, but with Trevor straddling him, one cop crushing his wrist, and the other pointing a .45 at Andre's head, he relented. The gun dropped from his open hand.

The officer who had been standing on Andre's wrist kicked the gun toward his partner. He and Trevor rolled the would-be assassin over. Trevor deftly removed Andre's wallet and pocketed it before the officer cuffed Andre's hands behind his back. The other officer holstered his sidearm and helped Andre stand by pulling his handcuffs high up his back. After patting him down for other possible weapons, he escorted the prisoner to his squad car while reading his rights from the Miranda card.

Trevor plopped down on the edge of his bed. The remaining officer asked, "Sir, are you okay?"

Trevor needed medical attention but couldn't waste time checking into a hospital. He had to be at DNAY tonight. "Ribs," he managed to say.

"Sir, I'm Sergeant Cirullo. I'll request an ambulance." The officer radioed the request. "They should be here shortly, sir."

"Thanks. How?"

"We had a call. Fortunately, we were on the way back to the station. I'm glad we arrived in time."

Tiffany rushed in, ran to the bed, and hugged Trevor. "Thank God you're okay."

He winced and groaned. She released him.

"I'm sorry. He hurt you?"

Trevor smiled. "You saved my life. I owe you."

She sat next to him on the bed and squeezed his thigh. "You can thank me later."

Ms. Flynn attempted to escape while Karl shared his glorious vision with her. She leapt to her feet and rushed at him. With his sharp reflexes, he easily stepped aside at the last instant. As she went past him, off balance, Karl smashed the butt of his handgun into her shoulder.

She dropped so hard that her arms did little to break the fall. Her forehead struck the carpeted floor, and she moaned. He holstered his gun, picked her up, and threw her into his leather chair. He took the gun out and trained it on her chest then yanked the front of her blouse. The fabric ripped, exposing her navy lace bra. Ms. Flynn sat in the chair, staring numbly.

He slapped her across the face. Her tear-filled eyes focused on him. "As I said, there is one final matter requiring your attention." She looked up. Karl undid his belt and unbuttoned his trousers. He pulled his zipper down and then his pants. He grabbed a fistful of her red hair and pulled her head to him.

Ms. Flynn stared straight ahead — unmoving. "Do it." Karl looked down at her. The green eyes were dull, wet, and lifeless. Slowly, she obeyed, and Karl watched intently. The top curves of her ample breasts were visible when she pulled back and hidden when she moved forward.

Minutes passed. Karl focused but could not get an erection. Why couldn't he take his eyes off her damned breasts? Karl became more and more frustrated.

"If you can't pleasure me this way, get up!" he shouted and pulled her out of the chair. She stood as if in a stupor. "Take off your skirt." She complied. "And those," he ordered, pointing his weapon at the matching navy panties. She wore only her high heels, suit jacket, and the ripped blouse, which revealed her bra and the curves of her excessively large chest.

The CEO gripped his assistant by one of her triceps and dragged her around to the side of the desk closest to his office door. He turned her, so she faced the desk then thumped her head into the blotter.

Karl saw the jacket draped over her back, the curves of her buttocks, and her soft thighs. Concentrating on her backside, he reflected on all the men he had killed one by one at his cabin. In less than twenty-four hours, he would exterminate the rest in one fell swoop. He would break the seal and bring the wrath of God to the vile, disgusting queers once and for all.

Karl's manhood was now fully engorged, and he was ready to sodomize his assistant. She screamed in pain, but Karl didn't care. His left hand pulled her hips to him while the butt of his gun rested on her right shoulder, the muzzle pressed against the lower portion of her head.

Like an athlete mentally preparing for a game, Karl contemplated tomorrow, with each detail going exactly as planned. The control test group survived while the contaminated subjects died an agonizing death. Karl pictured himself wearing his best black suit, shirt, and tie. The security force eliminated the lab techs and all of the scientists except Professor Garrett and his assistant, Menendez. Karl walked around the room. He passed the living subjects then the dead. He reached the wall and turned, so he could continue along the perimeter. He walked past the armor coated ductwork, turned along the back wall, opened the door, and went up the stairs. He observed the two testing chambers below from behind the bulletproof shielding at the master control panel. Karl initiated the sequence and released the vapor. Within days, the winds carried it across the country and throughout the world. It was still lethal when it reached Europe, Asia, and Africa.

Imagining countless homosexuals lying dead throughout the world, Karl tensed every muscle in his body and climaxed. As he did, his trigger finger clenched. The Sig fired pointblank into his assistant's skull, sending brains and bits of her head flying across the desk.

Karl pulled up his slacks and fastened his belt. He jotted a quick note advising the cleaning person to "Dispose of properly and make the office presentable."

The CEO shut down his computer and began to leave. He paused, remembering why he'd returned to his office this evening. He went to his coat tree and gathered his dry cleaning. Thank God for the plastic bags—he would never have been able to get a new custom-made black suit in time to wear tomorrow.

INTRUDER ALERT

Sergeant Cirullo verified Trevor's identification and took some quick notes for his report before he left.

Trevor wrote Tiffany a large check and asked her to let him get some rest before the ambulance crew arrived. She resisted and offered to make him feel better in her own ways. She didn't leave until the medics arrived.

They tried to order Trevor to go to the hospital for examination and treatment. He refused. Finally, they gave him a cursory examination, wrapped his ribs, and responded to their next call.

It was after seven o'clock, and Trevor was finally alone. He still hadn't heard from Lyn. He called her home and cell numbers but only got voicemail. He didn't leave any messages. He tried her office phone. Voicemail. He ended the call. *She wouldn't still be in Karl's office, would she?* If Trevor went in and did set off an alarm, he could be putting her in danger. *What if she was in trouble?* He decided to get ready and go in. If she wasn't in trouble, she should already be out of there. If she was in trouble, he might be in time to help.

He changed as quickly as possible with his injured rib. He threw on a loose-fitting black shirt. He leaned over to change socks, but the pain in his side slowed him. He pulled on black jeans and worked the thick black belt through the loops. His side burned as if it were on fire when he attached the waistband holster.

Trevor strapped on the shoulder holster. He pulled each of the two clips out of the pouch below his right arm and made sure they were at capacity before replacing them.

He took one pistol from the safe, looked over the top of the rear sight, and confirmed the red indicator showed a round in the chamber. He depressed the magazine release and verified nine rounds were loaded. Pleased with the results, he placed his left thumb over the striker panel and slid the handgun into the suede lined holster behind his back. Satisfied that it was snugly in place, Trevor examined the matching .45. The agent inserted the weapon securely into the shoulder holster and set the rig's thumb break.

He looked through Andre's wallet. He found a DNAY keycard and placed it in his right rear pocket. It hurt, but he could move that far. He took the cash out of Andre's wallet, added it to what was already in his money clip, and shoved the clip in his left front pocket.

He opened the carton Tiffany had accepted from DSL. An envelope rested on top of two parcels. He opened the envelope and removed a nondescript keycard. The card's magnetic stripe was programmed and treated, so it would mirror the last card swiped through a reader. All Trevor had to do was make sure he had the card lined up correctly when he used it. He placed it in his wallet to be certain he didn't mistake it for Andre's card.

Trevor then removed the smaller of the two remaining items. It was an electronic device that could be plugged into a retinal scanner. With any luck, it would dupe DNAY's system into unlocking the door to Karl's office.

The final item was a small parcel addressed to the President of DNAY from his local congressman. Although it appeared tightly taped shut, Trevor tugged at the box's right panel. The Velcro made a ripping sound as it released, and the flap pivoted down on the thin rod that served as a hinge.

The device inside was a small yet powerful incendiary bomb. Karl Joseph had to be behind both of the attempts on his life, as well as the death of Doctor Singh. Trevor would not feel bad about executing him, but he couldn't justify burning down the lab and possibly killing innocent employees. He'd only consider using the bomb if he was in dire straits. He could either set it to explode when the timer counted down to zero or to blow if someone opened the packaging. He couldn't get it in through the front door because the metal detectors would alert security. However, if he went in the back, he could most likely smuggle the bomb into the building undetected. He set the timer for ten seconds, leaving the bomb switched off. Ten seconds wouldn't give him enough time to escape, but he'd only use the bomb in an emergency situation anyway.

The agent clipped his cell phone to his belt and slipped on the black leather jacket. He put the retinal scanner override device in his left jacket pocket.

Going to the mirror, he made certain his outer shirt covered his rear gun, and the shoulder rig was not obvious when the jacket was zipped halfway up his chest.

Trevor's thoughts turned to the best way to breach DNAY's security measures. He noticed his reflection in the mirror. The normally good-humored eyes were hard, and his grin was gone. His face was now cruel, set with grim purpose. He gathered his equipment and hurried out of the hotel.

Trevor turned off his headlights well before he reached the DNAY building and cracked his window, so he could better hear if someone was patrolling the grounds. He drove around to the rear slowly enough that anyone working inside would not hear his approach. He parked his Highlander in the dirt behind the large dumpster. It was at an angle, so it should not be visible to anyone, even if they were taking trash to the dumpster. He unclipped his cell phone. He leaned over to set it in the glovebox and was promptly reminded of his broken rib.

At this time of night, both the security door and the delivery gate were closed as he had anticipated. Trevor patted himself down to be sure he had both his guns and the extra clips. Trevor took the car keys out of the ignition and dropped them into the center console. He placed a few CDs on top of the keys before closing the console panel. It was a quick job but should hide them from a casual inspection if anyone found and entered the vehicle. He couldn't risk the keys or the audible lock alerts making noise and giving him away. Besides, if they remained in the SUV, he wouldn't lose them. He stepped out of the vehicle. With the window slightly ajar, the door closed quietly.

Trevor leaned around the dumpster. There was no one in sight and no time to waste. Trevor was determined to discover what was going on inside.

He reached the back door, ignored the pain, and pulled Andre's keycard out of his rear pocket. The agent ran the card through the reader and was rewarded by a green light and the click of the bolt releasing. He held the door ajar, shoved the keycard back into his pocket, and removed the SW99 from his shoulder holster. He pressed against the side of the building and cracked the door enough to peer inside. From the limited nighttime lighting, he could see the way was clear. He was in!

He slid the gun into the holster and made his way quietly across the deserted loading bay area. There were only a few crates and boxes, all stacked neatly along the far wall. He turned on a row of overhead lights and darted to the other side of the bay to examine the stacked containers. He recognized some of the chemical names and equipment from his high school chemistry class, but they meant nothing to him. For all he knew, the items could be something every genetics lab required.

Trevor picked up one of the crowbars used to open the crates. If it came to close quarters combat, the weapon would be quiet, but it would also be lethal. He'd only use it for threat value unless his life was at stake. Until he knew what was going on, he didn't have any reason to kill the guards he'd come across. For all he knew, they might strictly be here to prevent terrorism or scientific espionage. He moved behind the forklift with his back to the wall and worked his way toward the corridor that led into the main building.

Trevor had to duck as he neared the doorway because of the industrial circuit breaker boxes mounted against the wall. He made a mental note that they were not locked in case the breakers could prove useful later. He looked into the hallway. Still clear. The nearest section was only lit by the nighttime lighting system. Farther ahead, the building was fully illuminated. He turned the row of lights off and allowed his eyes to adjust to the dimness again. He'd take advantage of the dark while he could.

Trevor was at a disadvantage only knowing a basic layout of the building, but his general sense of direction guided his overall course. He hoped to surprise any guards he might encounter before they could sound an alarm or report his presence. If he could neutralize them individually, he could make his way to the elevators and emergency stairwell. From either he could get to Karl's office.

Would he discover DNAY's secrets? He had

better find some damning proof and determine what to do in short order.

Staying in the darkness along the wall, Trevor moved slowly and quietly across the tile. He reached the first door on his right. He discerned a shelf jutting out of the middle and figured it acted as a counter if the top half of the door was open and the bottom half remained closed. Perhaps a scientist would find something behind this very door that could shed light on Karl's scheme. Trevor wasn't a scientist, so he moved onward.

Trevor approached the first intersecting passage. The lights were on past the junction and also down the side passage. A rock radio station played. Trevor thought this hallway abutted the back of the main laboratory. Although the building was maintained at a comfortable temperature, Trevor's hands were sweaty. He took turns wiping them on his slacks. Nobody straight ahead. That way would lead to the lobby and elevators, but first he had to take care of anybody in this wing.

The agent crouched against the wall and listened. Hearing nothing but the music from the radio, he turned and inspected the empty hallway. There were two doors, both on the right-hand side of the hallway.

Just as he was about to enter the passageway, he heard footsteps and saw a shadow fall across the doorway of the lounge. A voice called out, "When I get back, I look at the magazines, and you make the rounds." Trevor dodged behind the wall. That was close. This must be the security wing. His heartbeat drowned out the other guard's response. Trevor knelt on one knee, kept the crowbar at the ready, and breathed in slowly to calm himself.

The guard rounded the corner without looking in Trevor's direction and headed for the lobby. Trevor kept his weapon at his side and followed the guard. When Trevor had adjusted the distance to his liking, he whispered, "Excuse me."

The puzzled guard whipped around to look behind him. Trevor jabbed the curved end of the crowbar into the man's abdomen, and the guard doubled over gasping. Trevor didn't want to kill the guard, so he merely whacked him in the neck with the side of his hand. The blow forced the guard to the floor. Trevor hoped any noise was obscured by the music. He checked to be sure the guard was unconscious.

The agent spun and looked down the corridor from the lobby side of the intersection. No alarm and no one running. *So far, so good.* The cameras would probably cover the area where the guard lie since it was so close to the security hub. Trevor hurried to the first door before anyone noticed the unconscious guard on the monitors.

Trevor stopped and looked inside. He didn't see anyone in the lounge. Entering the carpeted room, he saw the monitoring station and the back of a seated security man, who seemed to be bouncing his head in time with the song's drum line as he studied a men's magazine.

The agent dashed across the room yelling the jo

battle cry he'd developed during his martial arts training. The surprised sentry turned in his chair. By the time he understood what was happening and reached for his sidearm, it was too late. Trevor jumped and dropkicked the guard in the chest. The chair slammed against the console, and the guard slumped, trying to catch his breath. Trevor punched him in the face, and the man's eyes rolled up before he lost consciousness. The girlie magazine fluttered to the floor and landed with the centerfold facing up. Trevor noticed the spread. "No wonder you were distracted."

The guard's eyes fluttered open. Trevor slugged him in the face again, and the guard's head lolled to the side.

Two guards had been taken out temporarily. Were there more? Where? Trevor realized he was leaning against the bank of security monitors. He stood and scanned them for movement. There—just one more. In the lab. Trevor started through the lounge when a large locker caught his attention. He wondered what was inside but couldn't waste time since he knew where the last guard was, but only for the moment. Now that the other guards were taken care of, he would only need to be concerned about stealth until he confronted the last security man. Then, he could make as much noise as necessary. He left the crowbar in the lounge, pulled the SW99 from his shoulder holster, and ran as silently as possible after his target.

Trevor approached the lab and saw the sliding

doors had been left open. He stayed close to the wall, careful not to make any sounds that would give him away. When he got to the door, he dropped to one knee and pivoted, covering the portion of the room he could see with his .45.

Staying low, he entered the laboratory and quickly took in as much as he could. Straight ahead a console stood in the center. Beyond it were two rooms, some sort of isolation chambers, presumably for keeping test subjects separate from the scientists and one another. The chambers each had a large window facing into the lab. To Trevor's left was a huge ventilation duct. *To clear the air in a hurry if an experiment went wrong?* Otherwise that side of the room was empty. To his right were two more consoles, in line with the first one he had seen. He spotted the guard patrolling the far corner of the room.

Trevor darted to the nearest console and crouched. He slowed his breathing and heard the guard's steady steps as he approached. Trevor leaned out far enough to observe the man making his rounds.

Soon he would be between Trevor and the chambers at the rear of the lab. The agent changed his grip on the SW99, so he was holding the slide. The pistol's grip extended from his hand, butt first. The guard saw him, but Trevor had the advantage. He launched himself upward, and the butt of his gun struck the guard hard under the chin. Blood and teeth flew out of the sentry's mouth as he staggered backwards, arms flailing. Without giving the man a chance to recover, Trevor hit him with a left hook that made him crash into the console.

The agent lifted the man's head and confirmed that the punch had knocked him out. Trevor holstered his semiautomatic and examined the equipment the other man carried. First, he removed the nightstick, two-way, key ring, and sidearm from the unconscious man and slid them toward the right chamber, far out of reach. Then, he took the pair of handcuffs from the man's utility belt. He placed one around the man's wrist and the other around one of the console's legs. He wouldn't be going anywhere.

Trevor was pleased with himself for disabling the men without killing them but didn't know if he could expect the same consideration. With the guards unconscious, he had a small window of time where he'd have the building to himself.

He stepped into an open elevator and pushed the button to go up to the third floor. Lyn had been wrong. He did reach the elevators in spite of security. He hoped that was the only thing she had been wrong about.

Karl Joseph's office was easy to locate. It was not only the largest; it was the only one with a retinal scanner.

Trevor was sure Andre's keycard was not programmed to allow access, so he took out the special keycard he'd received from headquarters. He would only have one chance to duplicate the stripe of the last card used in the reader, so he had to be certain to keep the card straight when he swiped it through the slot. He also needed to be sure to slide the card through with the mirrored magnetic stripe facing the reader head. If he stuck the card in incorrectly, the plastic would disturb the residue on the surface of the magnetic head, and he would not be able to duplicate the necessary data. Once Trevor was positive he had the card aligned correctly, he swiped it through with a steady hand. The green light went on. *Almost in…*

He shoved the card into the inside breast pocket of his leather jacket and pulled the retinal scanner equipment from the coat's left pocket. The agent inserted the jack into the scanner's programming port, pressed the button, and hoped for the best. Instead, the scanner began flashing red, and a computerized voice repeated, "Intruder alert, intruder alert…"

TRAPPED

It would take time for anyone to respond to the "...intruder alert..." Trevor had triggered, but he hurried down the stairwell and to the front entrance. Neither his special keycard nor Andre's card would open the door. He rushed to the other end of the building. The security door wouldn't open, so he tried the loading bay gate. No luck. The alert must have locked down the facility. Apparently, it could now only be opened by someone on the outside.

He was trapped! He hadn't even learned the true purpose of the testing that would begin in the morning. He had his pistols and extra clips, but shooting his way out of the building wouldn't answer any questions.

What about the guard he'd handcuffed to the control console in the lab? Maybe he'd know something. No. It might be possible for one or two key people to keep an important secret but the entire security team? Never.

Trevor searched the dock area. He considered possible locations to hide but quickly dismissed each of them. *Of course!* He'd seen the perfect place to conceal himself. Not only would it be unlikely he'd be discovered, but he'd get to see the experiments as an added bonus.

KILL HIM

Karl Joseph stepped out of his Mercedes Benz, Sig in hand. He knew Agent Byrne was responsible for the alarm. Mr. Slaughter had obviously failed. Karl would deal with that problem later. It mattered little. Agent Byrne would not live to see Karl's triumph.

In mere hours, the world would be changed, and the building Karl stood before, along with the unlucky test subjects trapped inside, would be smoldering ashes and debris.

Mr. Virelli, DNAY's beefy receptionist, had his hand on the butt of his Colt Python as he walked over to meet his boss. He clipped his two-way radio phone to his belt. "Everyone's here except for Andre Slaughter, sir. He hasn't reported. The rest of us are ready to move in at your word."

"Mr. Virelli, if Mr. Slaughter arrives, be sure he leaves dead. Agent Byrne is somewhere inside. Take four of the men in from the rear of the building. I'll take the rest through the front. If we don't find him on the first level, your men will search the second and third floors one at a time. Shoot to kill."

"Yes, sir." He returned to the group of men waiting in the lot. Four followed him to the back of the building, and the others gathered near Karl.

Karl swiped his card, and the doors parted before

him. His men poured through the foyer. Red lights lit on the reception desk, and the computerized voice warned, "Weapons detected, weapons detected..."

The sentries fanned out across the atrium sweeping their pistols back and forth. Someone shouted, "Clear." One man remained to guard the main entrance. Another checked that the elevators were empty and shut off the power to each of the cars. The remaining men divided into two groups. Karl led one group back the corridor toward the security wing while the rest sprinted to the lab.

The Chief Executive Officer saw a man prone on the floor ahead and ordered a guard to investigate. The young man who went forward circled to the far wall and held his gun steady in a two-hand grip, aimed at his target's head. The target didn't move, so the young man continued forward. He went over and knelt down, finally lowering his weapon. He rolled the man over and called back, "It's Garcia. He's still alive. Repeat: Garcia is still alive." Realizing he was kneeling with his back to the intersection, he spun around, his weapon once more ready.

Karl and his detail came forward. Karl slapped the fallen man's face to bring him around. When his eyes began to focus, Karl demanded, "How many?"

The guard was still dazed and kept blinking. He started to answer but only coughed. Finally, he managed, "I only saw one."

Karl stood and aimed his Sig at the guard's head. "There is no excuse for your failure, Mr. Garcia." Karl squeezed his trigger. Mr. Garcia's punishment would serve as an example. That should motivate the men to find Agent Byrne.

Karl motioned for the man who discovered Mr. Garcia to continue to the loading dock. Karl took the other two into the hallway on his left. The wing contained the monitoring room and was the most defensible section of the building—except for his secure control room in the lab.

The men covered the two doorways and stormed into the break room ready to fire their weapons. "Oh my God! Pittman's down, too!" Karl waited, but there was no gunfire. His guards still lacked initiative. Karl didn't bother questioning Mr. Pittman before he executed him.

Agent Byrne had secured the monitoring room. Why would he abandon it? Karl strode to the break room and checked the weapons locker. It was locked. He took a key from his pocket and opened it. None of the submachine guns was missing. Karl's timetable was too important to allow any disruption. He refused to allow the men to carry SMGs before the test subjects were all accounted for. The subjects wouldn't think twice about the handguns but might be frightened of anything larger. They could not be scared off.

Everyone's two-way crackled to life. "This is Walker. Greene is handcuffed to one of the consoles in the lab."

"Is he alive, Mister Walker?"

"Yes, sir. He was attacked, but he should be fine."

"Was the upper level of the lab breached?"

The silence did not last long but seemed to stretch out unbearably. "No, sir. Upper level secure."

Karl spoke slowly and annunciated clearly into his two-way, so the entire security team would understand his message. "Gentlemen, Mr. Garcia and Mr. Pittman are dead. My team will clean things up at our end. Mr. Walker, does Mr. Greene know Agent Byrne's whereabouts?"

After a short time, Mr. Walker responded, "No, sir."

"Then escort Mr. Greene to the dumpster and eliminate him for his failure to stop Agent Byrne."

A weak reply came over the speaker, "Yes, sir."

Karl ordered his men, "We must find and kill Agent Byrne before the subjects begin to arrive. We're running out of time. Try not to make a mess."

THE GATHERING

Ray Peters opened his door. Mo Jenkins rushed through the doorway. "Hey, you ready to go? We've got to be there before ten."

Ray rubbed his head. "Do I look ready? Have a seat. Give me a few minutes."

Mo turned off the TV and sat on the couch. "We're getting good money for showing up this morning. I don't want to be late and miss out. This will cover my credit card balance and a good dinner or two."

Ray walked back to his bedroom. He liked Mo, but the guy was damned annoying. Shows up an hour early wearing dress slacks and a button-down checked shirt. It's not even a frigging job interview; it's a guinea pig call. At least he wasn't wearing a tie. Ray threw on a tattered long-sleeve pullover and well-worn blue jeans. The woven brown belt he removed from the pile of laundry in the corner had seen better days, long ago when he had a decent job at one of the now-forgotten dotcoms. He pulled on a dingy pair of socks and slipped on his worn boat shoes. At least he'd be comfortable hanging out this weekend whether Mo was or not.

"Ok, I'm ready. Let's walk." Ray wanted to avoid eviction a little longer. He wasn't concerned about credit card bills or expensive meals. Chase had already charged off his credit card balance, and McDonald's value menu might not be high-class cuisine, but it was filling. He grabbed a ragged jacket off a wall hook and zipped it around him.

Mo offered, "I can pay our bus fare if you'd rather not walk."

Ray shrugged. "Enclosed spaces. People pressed up against me. No thanks. We have plenty of time. The walk will do us good."

Now Mo shrugged. "Whatever."

Deanne Baker tried to scream, but no sound came out of her mouth, only blood. She woke with a start. She couldn't recall the nightmare. Was it related to the experimental treatment she'd receive this morning? What was there to be nervous about? If the testing didn't go well, she'd end up with a headache or maybe diarrhea. She told herself everything would be okay, but she couldn't stop shivering.

She enjoyed a hot shower. Relaxed now, she went back to her room and picked out a blouse and skirt that didn't hide too much of her body. Wanting to be comfortable, she skipped the bra and wore flats rather than heels.

Deanne went downstairs. Her mother set down her cup of coffee and the remote control then went over and hugged her. "Oh, honey. I hope this works."

Deanne smiled at her mom. "It's the first day of the rest of my life," she said. She remembered waking abruptly, and a chill ran up her spine, but she dismissed the premonitions. "See you next week, Mom. I love you. Take good care of Justin for me."

"This once, since it's so important. I love you, too." The taxi's horn blared. "Sounds like your ride's here. You have everything you need?"

Deanne already had her purse. She picked up today's classified section, folded it, and stuffed it into the purse. "All set. Thanks, Mom." She kissed her mother goodbye and went to the waiting taxi.

Other than the overcome guards discovered last night, there was no trace of Agent Byrne. Karl had expected the three executions would motivate the remaining men. However, the security team had searched throughout the building and come up empty. Perhaps Agent Byrne escaped during the search? Karl regretted his decision not to get the Dobermans. They would certainly have found and killed the agent. Animals were more effective hunters and killers than humans and cheaper too. Mr. Steele and Mr. Slaughter had been a waste of money when it came to killing Agent Byrne.

Karl had originally thought the large security force was overkill to protect DNAY, but now he wasn't sure. Why did Agent Byrne spare the DNAY guards when he could easily have eliminated them? Maybe he couldn't bring himself to kill? It no longer mattered. Agent Byrne would stay out of Karl's way, or the agent would die.

Karl paced in his office. There was nothing to do but wait. The three guards who had been put to death had been thrown into the dumpster, and the blood had been cleaned thoroughly from the tile. The CEO considered his carpet. It wasn't obviously blood, but a stain was visible, especially in the morning sun's bright light. The janitor hadn't worked a miracle but had at least cleaned up all the bits of the executive secretary's brain and skull as well as her body. Karl had chosen wisely when he ordered the industrial-sized dumpster.

He looked at his Rolex Oyster Perpetual watch. 9:35. He called the front desk, and Mr. Virelli informed him that only forty people had arrived. Exactly a dozen to go. "Notify me immediately when everyone has checked in and been escorted to the lab."

"Of course, Mr. Joseph."

Ray and Morgan reached the large building's front entrance just as a taxi pulled up. Ray pointed an attractive black girl out to Morgan as she exited the cab and paid the driver. Ray made Morgan wait until she got closer, so they could walk inside together.

The girl approached the two young men. She stopped a few steps down from them. "Hi, boys," she paused. "I'm Deanne. You here for the experiment, too?"

Morgan was somewhat timid around good-looking females, but his friend Ray wasted no time. He responded immediately. "I'm Ray. We wanted to check this out. It sounded important." Morgan smiled but didn't introduce himself.

"It sure does," she gushed. "Who's your friend, Ray?"

"He's Mo."

At this, Morgan stuck out his hand. "I prefer Morgan." *I did it again! Always so formal. Why can't I just relax and be natural? I'll die a virgin at this rate.* Deanne came up another step, leaned forward, and shook his hand with gusto. His eyes were drawn by the way her breasts bounced. Embarrassed, his head shot up, and he looked into her large brown eyes. He knew he was blushing. *God, this is so mortifying. Maybe I should just fly out to Nevada and hire a hooker since it's legal out there. I'd probably be too shy to talk to any of them and would fly back home carrying my virginity onto the plane like baggage.*

"What're you doing when this is over, Morgan?" she asked in a playful voice.

Morgan wasn't sure if Deanne was just being friendly or if she was interested in him. "I guess just walking Ray back to his place. Do you want to come along?"

"Sure. Maybe we could stop somewhere for coffee on the way," she suggested.

Morgan didn't think that Ray would want to spend any of his own money buying coffee so Morgan offered, "Okay, my treat."

Deanne said, "Great, it's a date." She walked past them and through the sliding doors. As they followed her inside, Morgan thought maybe this could be his lucky day. Ray interrupted his thoughts with another of his typically blunt remarks, "Nice ass, huh?"

* * * *

"All subjects have been shown to the lab, Mr. Joseph. They will be ready when you get there, sir," Mr. Virelli's voice called over Karl's intercom.

Karl stopped pacing. He walked around to the phone and held down the button marked 'Reception.' "Thank you, Mr. Virelli. I'll be there momentarily."

Karl looked around his office for what he anticipated would be the final time. Everything he would need had already been removed or remotely backed up. He realized the room was too neat. He randomly pulled a few files from his credenza and placed them in two piles on the top of his desk. He reached inside his custom suit and confirmed the Sig was nestled in the leather shoulder holster. He buttoned the middle button of his wool and cashmere jacket.

The CEO knelt on a clean portion of the carpet. Karl made the sign of the cross and began to pray. "God, the time has come. With your blessing, I shall rid the world of the homosexual plague. Use me for your greater glory. Amen." He made the sign of the cross again and stood. Karl Joseph straightened his tie and went to fulfill his destiny.

CUT THE DECK

Karl Joseph walked through the sliding doors of the laboratory as they parted for him, like peasants making way for royalty. He saw that the group of fifty-two test subjects had already been evenly divided into two groups. Cut like a deck of cards. After making a quick visual inspection, he presumed that the group to his left was the control group and those on his right were infected with the virus. Ultimately, it didn't matter. Neither group would leave the laboratory alive.

The CEO knew the subjects would expect a speech. Professor Garrett patiently discussed something with Technician Menendez. The other lab techs looked anxious. Had they known they would be eliminated following the experiment, they wouldn't have been in such a hurry for its conclusion. Shortly thereafter, DNAY would burn to the ground, and the surviving test subjects would be consumed by the blaze.

"Good morning. My name is Karl Joseph. I am the Chief Executive Officer and President of Research and Development at DNAY." He paused and considered for a moment. *Yes, I am smiling at them. Good.* "Thank you for taking time out of your busy schedules and hectic lives to provide us the opportunity for a human trial of our HIV and AIDS therapy."

He opened his arms wide and his smile became genuine. "It has long been my dream to eliminate this pestilence from the earth." His right arm swept the room. "The exceptionally intelligent geneticists and technicians you see here have unlocked secrets of the mysterious strands of life we call D...N...A.

"You are the brave men and women who shall forever be associated with this bold experiment. If we are successful, the world will owe you a debt of gratitude!"

He turned to one of the technicians. "And now, please escort these fine people to their chambers, so we may alter the future." The tech motioned for another to help him. They went to the far end of the lab, behind the groups facing Karl.

"This way, please," the first technician said as he pointed to the doorway of the isolation tank on the left side of the room. His counterpart was leading the other group to a similar but reversed chamber. Although the walls gave the impression of meeting in the middle, each room was separate and self-contained. From inside, the subjects could look out of their large window into the main lab, but they could not see into the other chamber.

The rooms had doors in the back marked as restrooms. Had someone tried to open one of these, he would have found it was only a façade. The doors did not open, and there was nowhere to go. The inexpensive sofas, chairs, and tables in the two rooms did not match. The only things they had in common were the fruit and punchbowls sitting on each table and the fact the furnishings were available for immediate delivery from a nearby discount warehouse.

Deanne called to Ray and Mo, "I'll see you guys later!"

Ray noticed that Mo only gave a weak wave, so Ray shouted across the room, "Yeah! It'll be great!" He followed Mo and told him, "I think she likes you."

Mo asked, "Really? Ray, I, uh, I don't know what to do."

Ray was about to give Mo a few pointers when he heard the door hiss into place behind him. He spun around. He realized he was locked in a tiny room for the rest of the weekend with Mo and two dozen strangers. His heartbeat quickened. He began to sweat. "Mo, I can't do this. I need out."

"Ray, we're here until this experiment is over. Relax. We're all in this together."

Ray nervously looked around the room. The men and women trapped with him came from various ethnic backgrounds: Black, Asian, Indian, Hispanic, White. What did he have in common with them? Ray felt as if the tiny room started to shrink. The walls seemed to close in on him. "That's the problem..."

The technicians carefully completed their checklists and verified the status indicators and dials on their boards. Professor Garrett ambled over to Karl and told him everything was in order. "We only await your instructions."

Karl's skin tingled with excitement. He was about to redirect the world's future. "Open the intercoms to the isolation rooms."

Professor Garrett relayed the command, "Menendez, open intercoms to the subjects."

Menendez looked over the top of her glasses and flipped two switches up. The nervous chatter coming from the people in the tanks became audible. "Intercoms engaged, sir."

Karl stood behind his associate and placed both hands firmly on the man's shoulders. "Professor Garrett, you deserve the honor. Whenever you are ready."

The scientist turned and looked at the CEO with gratitude. Professor Garrett's face beamed like a child's when told he could open one of his Christmas presents on Christmas Eve rather than wait until the next day. He held out his hand. Karl accepted, and they shook hands. Professor Garrett warmly said, "Thank you," then strode purposefully to his control panel and stopped before the red buttons labeled "A" and "B." He flipped aside the plastic safety covers.

THE VENGEANCE OF THE LORD

From his hidden vantage point within the laboratory's large ventilation shaft, Trevor clearly saw the profiles of both his primary targets: Karl Joseph and Charles Garrett. This could be his best opportunity to stop them, but he still didn't know their plan. Karl's words sounded harmless, yet the speech held a sinister overtone—or was it only Trevor's imagination? Besides, if he killed them now, he was a sitting duck. No, he'd wait a little longer. He could observe both isolation tanks although he could not see the subjects near the dividing wall in the far chamber.

Professor Garrett solemnly pressed buttons A and B simultaneously. Karl Joseph spoke, "And the vengeance of the Lord will come like a thief in the night."

Deanne was thinking of Justin when she raised her face to the fine mist spraying from nozzles in the ceiling. Someone near her screamed hoarsely and Deanne turned. Deanne's nose and throat became horribly raw. Each shallow breath burned all the way down into her lungs. Her heart pumped boiling oil. Her skin prickled, about to blister. Everyone she saw was grabbing his or her throat and falling to the floor.

Deanne touched the scorching blood streaming

from her nose. She tried to scream. The only sound was the gurgling that accompanied her spewing blood. She was living her nightmare. A man beat at the door until he collapsed in a pool of blood and urine. Deanne's bladder and bowels released. Her bodily waste was fire against her legs. Her eyes closed. They refused to open. Deanne fell. Her head slammed against the floor. Deanne no longer cared. The warm, white light was calling her home.

Ray heard a gruff scream and pounding coming from the adjacent chamber but didn't know what to make of it. A mist fell on Ray and the others. They were damp but unharmed. Had the experiment failed?

Ray couldn't worry about it right now. He shouted, "Let me out! I need out!" His hands were already sore, but he continued to slap the door and window with his open palms. They had to see him. They had to let him out.

Trevor Byrne couldn't see the ghastly deaths of all twenty-six subjects in the far chamber, but he had seen more than enough. He sagged against the vent's grille, puking and gagging.

He was vaguely aware of Garrett reaching into his lab coat and pulling out something small. The professor hurled it at him. Trevor barely brought his hands up to shield his face before the vial shattered against the duct. He couldn't focus. Reflexively, he struck out at the grille. It fell inside the lab, and he crumpled over the duct's lower edge. He had no recollection of the security guards rushing into the room and pulling him from the shaft or taking him to wait outside the CEO's office for his arrival.

Karl Joseph gloated. "Success! Professor Garrett, you've unlocked God's code. Now, I can fulfill my purpose and implement His plan."

Karl turned to Technician Menendez. "Turn off the microphones and speakers in the isolation chambers." When the noise coming from the control tank on the left stopped, he gathered Professor Garrett and Technician Menendez to him. They distanced themselves from the others.

"Ladies and gentlemen, thank you for your support and dedication. The professor, his assistant, and I are about to improve the world. Your help has been invaluable. Now, I have a surprise for you."

A security team armed with submachine guns burst into the lab. Gunfire thundered and echoed, drowning out the ungrateful screams of the slaughtered technicians.

Karl commended the assault team, "Good work men. Dismissed." The team withdrew. Karl addressed his remaining associates, "Begin the final preparations. I won't be gone long."

Karl left the lab, unconcerned with the bodies strewn across the floor and the still-living test subjects behind him. The one man in the building who would have cared about them had been drugged, captured, and disarmed, and he wouldn't be alive much longer.

GOD'S WILL BE DONE

Trevor returned to consciousness and became aware that he was being held up by two of the security detail. His eyes slowly focused, and he saw Karl seated behind a large desk. Like Trevor, Karl was dressed entirely in black. However, the CEO had obviously spent more time and money on his custom-made ensemble than Trevor had when selecting his own clothing off the racks. Trevor had to admit Karl's sense of fashion was impeccable.

Trevor forced himself to relax and began to take in his surroundings. In addition to two small stacks of files on the desk, Trevor spotted his shoulder holster with his primary weapon and the two spare clips lying on the blotter. His leather jacket hung from one of the pegs on the coat tree.

He suddenly realized that he saw *one* of his SW99s on the desktop. He breathed in deeply, as if to clear his head. At the same time, he pushed his stomach outward against his belt. The guards had taken the obvious weapon but overlooked the one hidden inside his waistband! With only the one clip, he wouldn't make it past the entire security team and out of the building, but if he could get the guards to loosen their grip, he might be able to grab the weapon and spare clips four yards away. He'd need to distract them.

"Agent Byrne, welcome to my office. I'd ask you to have a seat, but you won't live long enough to remember my lack of manners."

Trevor tried to speak, but nothing came out at first. Karl was amused and motioned for him to continue. After a brief coughing fit, the agent was able to ask, "What happened in there? What are you doing?"

Karl checked his Rolex and sat back. He had time to kill. "I'm carrying out God's will, Agent Byrne. Historically, God had to mete out justice Himself. The rampant homosexuality that has continued to spread throughout the centuries is repulsive in His sight. Although He destroyed cities like Sodom and Gomorrah, the depravity lingered and grew. Eventually, He created the HIV virus to eliminate them all. Although it killed many, I knew that HIV wasn't the final answer."

The tall blond man stood and walked to the front of his desk, standing between Trevor and his goal. "Instead, it was *the key*! We have found a way to use the virus to trigger a catalyst. When an otherwise harmless combination of chemicals and genetic material comes in contact with someone infected by HIV, it sparks a reaction that destroys the body from within. We've even discovered that if a healthy subject contacts bodily fluid from an infected subject while the catalyst is still active, it will cause the reaction in the healthy subject's system as well."

The executive was clearly enthusiastic and clearly

psychotic. Trevor could still see the innocent people dying in the chamber. He'd never completely erase the memory. "What about all the test subjects you killed today? How could you stand there and watch them die?"

Karl replied, "Death dealt the hand, Agent Byrne. I merely cut the deck."

The CEO continued, "You see, the remaining twenty-six test subjects cannot leave their isolation chamber for three days. The doors have been set with a time lock. In a few minutes, I will return to the lab and release a large enough supply of the vapor to spread throughout the world within its eleven day potency period. Once the vapor has been released, the compressor that forces air through the ventilation system you were found hiding in will keep running. After it purifies the air in the lab, it will literally burn itself out. The excessive supply of flammable chemicals stored in opened containers in the compressor room will combust when the flames reach the fumes. This entire building will be destroyed, and those men and women trapped in isolation will be cremated. It will appear as though we had an unfortunate accident while running our tests. Because everything will be consumed by the fire, no one will realize the infected group was already dead."

Trevor wasn't sure Karl was right. With all of the forensic tools available today, investigators might be able to determine that the one group had been killed prior to the fire. Then again, if it burned long enough and hot enough, maybe there wouldn't be enough left to examine.

Karl leaned against the edge of his desk. Although well-concealed by the expert tailoring, Trevor detected the shoulder harness Karl wore. "Do you know how rampant HIV is in third world countries, Agent Byrne? Asia, India, and Africa have been hit hard by the virus. Think how glorious it will be. All of the vile minorities that will be purged. And we all know how emotional they are. They'll fall all over their dead loved ones weeping. Then, they'll die too." Karl laughed the laugh of the insane.

"Once I've eradicated HIV and AIDS, the worldwide job market will open considerably. If everyone who will die had been gainfully employed, there would be more than fifty million vacancies, counting all those who will die by secondary contact. However, that number includes all the crack heads and welfare recipients who do nothing to contribute to society. Not only shall I implement God's will, I shall eliminate unemployment. My backers are prepared to transfer land holdings from those who die to the highest bidders. I will receive a modest commission from each auction. There may even be a Nobel Prize in my future. What do you think, Agent Byrne?"

The agent could hardly believe what he'd just heard. "Whatever the reason those people were infected by HIV, they have just as much right to life as everyone else. You may be close to preventing HIV or curing AIDS, but that's not what you want. What do I think, Karl? I think you're a bigot and a closet homosexual. Because of your religious upbringing, you're disgusted by homosexuals. You can't admit to yourself that you are one. By killing as many gay men as you can, you hope to eliminate temptation and obtain absolution."

Karl's face reddened, and the veins in his neck stood out. He closed the space between himself and the agent and pummeled Trevor. The security men held their prisoner tightly as blow after blow landed. Trevor's broken rib was struck again and again. He could hardly breath, hardly stand. His face and body were battered and bruised. Blood streamed from above his left eye. Finally, the beating stopped.

The CEO composed himself as he walked to his washroom and cleaned his hands. "I will give you credit, Agent Byrne. You managed to get past several members of my security force. They were executed for their failure. Their comrades here will repay you. I would kill you myself, but I have more important matters to attend."

"Would killing me personally violate your fundamental Christian beliefs?"

Karl's eyes narrowed at Trevor's carefully chosen words. He understood the comment's wording was intentional. He punched Trevor in the jaw. Blood spurted from the agent's mouth. Karl adjusted his jacket and tie. "I must go, Agent Byrne."

Karl picked up Trevor's shoulder holster and headed for the door. Trevor tried to shout at him, but the words were muffled by his cut and swollen lips. He struggled against the viselike grips of his captors to no avail.

Karl turned. "I do have one more piece of information that may interest you, Agent Byrne. See that?" Trevor tried to focus on the oddly shaped dark stain on the carpet where Karl pointed. "You shouldn't have asked your whore girlfriend to spy for you. She wasn't nearly as good at spying as she was at sex."

Trevor knew now was not the time for regret. Mercifully, the guards allowed him to fall to his knees. He threw his hands up to his face, apparently in grief, but actually to wipe the blood from his eyes. Karl ordered his men, "When you are finished with him, throw him in the dumpster. Then, he can be with his bitch." The executive left the eager men to their task.

Either the men weren't armed, or they wanted to enjoy themselves. The guard who had been holding Trevor's left arm stepped closer and raised his foot. As the heavy boot approached the back of Trevor's head, Trevor rolled forward and onto his back. The man stretched to reach him but missed. When the guard's foot came down and all of his weight was on the forward leg, Trevor kicked, and his heel shattered the man's kneecap. The security man grabbed his knee and fell to the floor in excruciating pain.

The other man saw Trevor had more fight left in him than he'd expected. He allowed Trevor to rise while he kept his distance. Trevor stayed clear of the man on the floor and circled closer to his standing opponent. Trevor couldn't see well through the blood running into his eye. He could ignore the pain but not his impaired sight.

Trevor saw the man coming for him, but didn't see the fist until it was too close to avoid. He barely had time to duck his head, so the blow would land on his forehead rather than his eye. The impact jarred his head, and he was too slow to dodge the left cross that followed. He stumbled to the desk and worked his way around the other side to put some space between them.

He wiped the blood out of his eye again and saw a weapon he had not considered. Trevor lunged for the coat tree. He picked it up and swung it at his adversary. The security man threw up his arm to block the heavy object. Trevor heard the satisfying sound of breaking bone. The man's useless left arm hung at his side. The man threatened, "You son of a bitch. You're dead."

Trevor grunted. The man snarled and rushed at him. Trevor anticipated the dropkick. He sidestepped and leveled the coat tree down across his foe's face. The guard's head bounced off a corner of the desk, and Trevor knew that the neck had snapped even before he saw the final, awkward tilt of the man's head against his chest.

The guard with only one functioning knee crawled to Trevor. The agent didn't want to shoot the man since the sound would attract attention, but he didn't have time to waste. He picked up the nearest chair and brought it down hard on his opponent's unprotected skull. The man's face slammed into the floor and blood gushed from his nose. Trevor didn't stop to see if the man was alive or dead.

Trevor picked up his jacket and threw it on. He hurried to the sink in the washroom. Trevor rinsed the blood from his face and mouth then ran more cool water across his swollen lips. He held his palm tightly against the cut above his eye to staunch the flow of blood. When Trevor was satisfied the blood had slowed enough that he would be able to see, he noticed how bad he looked. The face in the mirror showed no hint of the young and carefree Petey, only a determined and battered man. Battered, but not beaten! Trevor went to the elevator.

He pressed the elevator's call button and waited. How much time did he have to stop the madmen? What about the remaining security force? How many were left? He had only ten .45 caliber rounds at hand. He'd need to acquire some of the guards' ammo or weapons if he was to stand a chance of getting out alive. At all costs, he must execute Joseph and Garrett before they release the vapor. If he could stop them and destroy the lab equipment, no one else should be able to duplicate the poison. That was critical even if he had to sacrifice himself. Where the hell was the elevator?

The indicator was lit, but Trevor jabbed the call button again. As he did, he noticed movement in the mirrored surface of the metal plate. The agent spun around. The guard whose knee had been shattered was coming at the agent with a sharpened, dual-edged letter opener. The guard was holding the weapon with one hand and pulling himself forward with the other. Trevor's first instinct was to kick the blade away, but instead he circled around the man on the ground. The man turned. Trevor lunged and grabbed the wrist holding the letter opener. The agent pulled the man's arm up, lifted his leg, and brought it straight down into the guard's shoulder. The crunch was as horrible as the guard's scream of agony. The dislocated arm fell at an unnatural angle. A chime announced the elevator had arrived at last.

Trevor removed the weapon from the guard's useless hand. Grabbing a fistful of the man's oily hair, Trevor lifted the man's head and used the blade to cut deeply into his carotid artery. Trevor stepped back as the blood spurted out in time with the man's dying heartbeat. This sentry would not surprise him again. The elevator doors were already closing, and Trevor just managed to edge his shoulder between the doors and push them apart. Once inside, he hit the "G" button for the main floor. Trevor stood in the front corner of the elevator, near the number panel, in case any of the remaining sentries were waiting below. In retrospect, the stairs would have been a better choice.

The elevator chimed again, and the doors slid apart. There was no gunfire, so the agent leaned out to take a look. Two sentries were visible, walking away. Trevor stepped out of the elevator and continued to work his way to the lab.

He crouched at the nearest corner when he heard footsteps approaching. A bullet entered the wall where his head had been. Staying in a crouch, he sprinted to one side and saw the lone guard who had fired at him. The guard must have been inexperienced because he remained in the same spot while he tried to reacquire the agent. Trevor was calm from years of experience. He fired, and the hollowpoint burst through the sentry's chest. The guard yelped and stumbled before falling onto what remained of his back with a final thud.

Trevor wondered how many security men remained. One was likely at the monitors. The rest must be roaming the facility. The agent crept along the wall until he reached the corner of the corridor leading to the lab. He felt the pull of his objective but remained calm and professional. Three men guarded the entrance. They were wearing police holsters and armed with handguns.

He knelt near the corner and leaned into the corridor. His left arm was extended and sideways to his target. He squeezed the trigger slowly and held it in as he heard the gunshot and felt the recoil. Before the men could reach their weapons and bring them into position, Trevor released the trigger and squeezed again. He ducked back behind the wall.

Trevor heard one man cry out and another grunt before he fell. Two down. The remaining guard fired three shots, but they all missed.

Trevor gritted his teeth and rolled into the passageway. He aimed his SW99 at the remaining guard's chest. The young man looked at Trevor stupidly, dropped his weapon, and put his hands in the air over his head. The youth targeted in Trevor's sights said, "I surrender."

Trevor didn't have time for either prisoners or sympathy. He fired, and the round passed cleanly through the young man's heart. He fell to the floor clutching his chest in disbelief.

Trevor approached the lab and didn't see anyone through the doors. The agent continued forward, and the doors slid open. Two guards spun around. Trevor fired twice at the closer of the two and dove from the doorway back into the corridor. He heard one guard fall to the floor and the other run.

Trevor pressed himself into the corner where the door's frame and the wall met. The sentry stood inside the doorway and fired a burst from his submachine gun. The noise echoed loudly inside the lab. The guard hadn't seen where his target had gone but was sweeping the passage in an attempt to cut him down. The man stepped through the doorway and stopped. Before he could spot his target, Trevor shot him. The hollowpoint left a gaping hole in the far side of the man's neck as it exited. The SMG dropped to the floor, followed by the dead man's body.

Trevor hurried into the lab hoping he still had time to stop Karl. He saw one of the technicians, probably Menendez, working at a console. He kept his gun trained on her as he scrutinized the area. She paused what she was doing and studied him.

The lifeless bodies of the other technicians littered the floor. He looked quickly at the living captives in the isolation room. Because of the time lock, he couldn't do anything for them yet. He felt sorry for the somehow familiar looking young man jumping around inside and pounding his bloodied fists on the window. Trevor noticed Menendez glance toward the upper rear of the lab.

Trevor looked up and realized there was a second level built along the rear of the lab. He'd missed it before because the reinforced entrance on the ground level blended in so well with the rest of the lab's design. He ran to the door. It was locked, and he didn't have the code.

Trevor perceived a faint hum as one of the speakers was reactivated. "Agent Byrne, you truly amaze me! It seems our destinies are intertwined." Karl laughed abruptly. "Like strands of DNA!"

KARL'S ULTIMATE SECRET

Without letting the technician out of his sight, Trevor backed into the room in order to see better. He saw a small room surrounded by a wall of glass that ended several feet above Karl and Garrett's heads.

"You can put your gun away, Agent Byrne. I have left nothing to chance. Professor Garrett and I are protected by bulletproof glass. Anyway, from that angle you wouldn't have a clean shot."

The technician spoke, "Professor, I'm done down here. I'm coming back up now."

Karl answered for the scientist, "Thank you, Technician Menendez. Please remain below and keep our guest occupied."

Menendez nervously glanced around the lab and suddenly bolted for the hallway. The loud crack of Trevor's gunshot was followed by Menendez's wail. She tumbled to the floor, her right knee shattered by the round. Trevor ordered the crippled technician, "Not so fast." He tuned out her cries when the CEO spoke.

"When I flip this switch, the vapor will be pumped from our underground storage tank, through the ductwork to your left and into the polluted Middletown air!

"Who is worthy to break the seal? I release the

rider on the pale horse, and his name is Death. And he was given power over a fourth of the world to kill by plague!" Karl shouted triumphantly. Trevor heard the click when Karl flipped the switch.

Trevor knelt behind the nearest console and was promptly reminded of his broken rib. He winced, exhaled. He focused his attention along the wall to his left. He spotted a slim, rectangular duct marked with alternating red and yellow hash marks painted at evenly spaced intervals from floor to ceiling. He fired. Ping. The hollowpoint was deflected and fell harmlessly to the floor.

"Agent Byrne, the duct work is armor plated. I took no chances. You've failed."

The agent was down to his last round. An armor-piercing round! He took a deep breath. With no time left, Trevor lined up the front sight of the SW99 with the shaft. Everything came down to this final moment. Trevor exhaled slowly and squeezed the trigger. He heard the shot and felt the recoil. The slide locked open on his empty pistol. He released the trigger. The bullet penetrated the shielding with a thud that was immediately followed by a high-pitched hiss. Trevor saw a pale mist spray from the shaft into the room.

Karl roared, "No!"

Trevor stood and depressed his pistol's slide release. It might be empty, but the steel slide would hurt like hell if it caught someone in the face. The agent rotated his grip on the butt of his pistol, so the slide rested along the outside of his forearm, and he could use the pistol like a short police baton.

Karl raced to the bottom of the stairs. He leaned against the door, a look of dread on his face. He stepped through the doorway clutching his throat and reaching out for his enemy. He staggered closer to Trevor.

Blood rushed out of Karl's nose, mouth, and ears. Trevor had seen what the gas did to the victims trapped in their booth and instinctively avoided the dying man. Karl had told him if someone came into contact with poisoned bodily fluids while the catalyst was active it would affect him as well.

Karl lost control of his bladder just before his legs gave out, and he fell to the floor. Trevor didn't realize the smell would be so terrible. It was the stench of death and decay. Karl rolled onto his side in a puddle of his own blood and waste then brought his legs to his chest in the fetal position. Karl's face twisted into a mask of agony and shame.

The agent watched Karl's body for what seemed like minutes. When he was sure Karl wouldn't rise for a final attack, Trevor holstered his empty pistol behind his back. "Choosing the black suit was the best decision you made today, Karl."

The hissing ceased and a mechanical drone began. "Shit!" The vapor was being sucked into the lab's ventilation system. It would be contained and merely circulated within the building. Trevor had stopped the poison from escaping for now but had forgotten about the impending fire. He had to find a way to shut down the compressor, or the captives would die, and the vapor would still be released!

There had to be a shutoff switch on the master control panel upstairs. Garrett was still up there. The scientist had earlier knocked Trevor out with a vial he'd thrown. What other tricks did he have in his lab coat? The agent gave Karl's body a wide berth, careful to avoid stepping in or touching any of Karl's bodily fluids, as he ran to the open door.

The stairs made a ninety degree angle up to his left after the bottom four steps. Making sure not to brush against the wall in case Karl had left any toxic oils or sweat behind, the operative leaned his head past the wall and looked up the stairway. The professor was busy pressing buttons and studying a display.

The mechanical drone became a whine. Trevor needed to hurry. He centered his weight and dashed up the stairs as quickly and quietly as he could. He was only two steps away from Garrett when the scientist's left hand came up aiming a small-caliber compact semiautomatic at Trevor's chest.

Garrett pressed some buttons and smiled smugly. "Well, it seems my employer had a few skeletons in his closet. Fortunately, he has already transferred the final payment to my account."

Trevor took the opportunity to solicit Garrett's help. "That's great news, Professor, but there are over two dozen innocent people down there that will die if we don't shut off the compressor. And if this building burns down, the toxin could still do its job. You don't want to be responsible for wholesale manslaughter, do you? If you shut down the compressor, I'll let you walk out of here."

The professor laughed deeply. "My work has killed so many over the years. If Karl was right and there is a God, I'm already condemned to hell. What difference does two dozen or even fifty million more make? I am the one holding the upper hand," he nodded to his pistol.

Garrett gathered several CDs and stuffed them into one of the lab coat's pockets. "I only accepted this job to see if I could create a biological weapon of this magnitude. I couldn't spend my retirement wondering if I would have solved the puzzle or not. I can now enjoy my retirement."

The professor swept the room with his hand and continued. "The compressor cannot be stopped. It was constructed to run continuously once started. I wouldn't really care if my vapor was unleashed or not. I know it works. However, if it puts your mind at peace before you die, the recirculation and purification system here has already neutralized the vapor's effects. When this building burns to the ground, the vapor will harm no one. You saved millions." Garrett smiled. "Unless I decide to sell the formula to another party."

Trevor gave him a deadly stare and bent his knees slightly to lower his center of gravity. "I can't let you do that."

Garrett replied, "You can't stop me." Trevor sprung forward. Garrett squeezed the trigger as Trevor grasped his wrist and pushed his arm off target. The bullet hit the wall, and the muzzle of Garrett's gun smashed through one of the monitor's screens, followed by Garrett's hand.

Trevor released his grip on the man's arm. Garrett yelled in pain. His hand was sliced by the glass, and electricity coursed through the pistol and up his arm. He dropped the small pistol, and it fell into the smoldering monitor. The scientist looked at his burned hand. Through the flow of blood, he must have seen one finger was nearly severed. He bellowed, "I'll kill you!" and threw a punch with his good hand.

Trevor blocked the punch. Garrett kicked out and struck Trevor's chest with his loafer. Trevor shouted and stumbled back into the wall. He reached behind his back and pleaded, "You've won. Stop."

Garrett picked up a hefty piece of equipment and closed the distance between them. "I won't stop until you're dead." He lifted the object over his head with both hands. Blood streamed down his arms.

Trevor's hand reached the butt of his pistol, and he jerked it out of the holster in the inverted grip he had used when Karl advanced on him downstairs. The agent pivoted and swung. The top of the .45's slide struck the scientist's jaw with devastating force. Garrett's head snapped back, and the piece of equipment he was brandishing dropped to the floor.

Blood, saliva, and teeth fell from Garrett's deformed mouth. He swayed. His eyes were unfocused but seemed to be searching for something or someone. Trevor grabbed the professor's lab coat from behind and helped him down the stairs. They reached the main floor when Trevor felt the scientist tense and reach for one of his pockets.

Garrett threatened, "If this test tube breaks, we are dead men." Unexpectedly, he threw it to the ground. It shattered.

Trevor spun Garrett, so they faced one another. He released him and stared. "Why?" Trevor noticed movement behind the scientist.

Garrett laughed. He turned but stumbled over Menendez, who had quietly crawled behind him. Trevor shoved him toward Karl's body. Garrett sprawled. He screamed, "No!" and tried to regain his balance but couldn't. One knee landed atop Karl's ankle, and the scientist's body continued forward. His bloody hand slid through the sticky pool, allowing Karl's bodily fluids to mix directly with the scientist's blood. Garrett's head smacked against the floor.

Menendez moaned, "The test tube was empty."

Trevor reached down and supported Menendez, so he could help her out of the lab. Trevor didn't want to witness what was about to happen but needed to be sure Garrett had been neutralized like his biological weapon. Trevor was amazed when the professor pushed himself up onto hands and knees and turned to face him.

The scientist's good humor had turned to insanity knowing the horrible death that would soon claim him. His misshapen smile was gruesome, and his wild eyes locked onto Trevor. The professor sounded like he was trying to clear his throat. Trevor guided

Menendez away. Garrett puckered his lips. Too late, Trevor realized what type of attack his enemy was preparing to launch.

Professor Garrett spit a reddish-black glob at the agent and collapsed. Trevor dived to one side, barely avoiding the lethal phlegm. Menendez collapsed. She wasn't so lucky. Garrett raised his head to see if he had hit the agent. He saw Menendez trying to wipe the glob from her face, her hands. She screamed in terror. Trevor stood at a safe distance and shook his head. Garrett's disappointment was evident before blood streamed out of his eyes and nose to join that already flowing from his mouth. Garrett's eyes closed for the final time, and his head fell to the floor.

Nausea threatened the agent. His mouth filled with saliva. It would be so easy to puke again. Just lean over. Among the other odors, he smelled ozone. The compressor's whine became an irregular grinding screech. The motor was burning itself out. Trevor could think of only one way to shut it down. He hurried from the room and fought the urge to vomit.

ALONG CAME A SPYDER

Trevor hurried to the rear of the building. He would turn off the circuit breakers. That would shut down the pump.

When he reached the circuit boxes, he opened the panels and immediately spotted the large red switches. Before throwing them to the off position, he opened the security door and propped it ajar with a small but sturdy box. He ran back and flipped both switches. The rear of the building became dark instantly except for the daylight spilling in from the open exit door.

Trevor needed to be sure no one would turn the power back on before Earl could have this part of the power grid shut down. He drew his gun. Holding the pistol by its slide, he used the butt to break the red switches off of the panels. That would do the trick.

Trevor walked over to the door and leaned down to move the box. A bullet struck the door above him. Trevor rushed outside and spun around. It was the ape, Tony. Trevor kicked the box into the room then flung the door shut. He heard the bolt automatically click into place. *Thank God!* Now Tony and whoever else remained were locked inside until the police or the FBI arrived on the scene.

Trevor was finally so near to Lyn, but he

hesitated when he reached the dumpster. He thought of the night they shared and opened the cold metal lid. He gagged from the reek but forced himself not to turn away. He rolled aside the three sentries who had been dumped without ceremony into the container and sifted through the waste. He threw bags and boxes onto the macadam until he found a heavy steel-colored plastic bag. He untied the knot, opened it, and looked inside. Lyn's body was missing most of its head.

He pounded his fists against the dumpster in anger and frustration. Finally, he put the rear seats of his SUV down, backed the vehicle around to the trash receptacle then opened the hatch to his cargo area. Ignoring the pain from his broken rib, Trevor lifted the bag with Lyn's lifeless body as gently as he could. He carried her to his SUV and placed her inside. He closed the hatch. He'd see that her body was laid to rest with the respect she deserved.

Trevor needed to report to Earl but wanted to get as far away from DNAY as he could. He climbed into the SUV and fidgeted in the seat. The feel and smell of death in the enclosed vehicle was overwhelming. He pushed the button to slide the moon roof completely open, and he lowered all four windows to circulate the crisp outside air.

He pulled away from the dumpster and had reached the side of the building when he heard reinforced glass shatter, followed by submachine gun bursts. *Now what?* He floored the accelerator and soon entered the front lot. The agent looked over at the building and saw that Tony and another man had used the SMGs to weaken and break one of the reinforced glass panels. Trevor ducked as a burst riddled the back half of his SUV's passenger side with bullet holes.

When the hail of lead stopped, Trevor sat up, saw he was heading for a parked car, and adjusted his course. He was at a serious disadvantage. His guns were empty, and he wasn't very familiar with the local roads or which ones might be busy. He made a sharp right out of the parking lot and turned onto Kreider Drive. He sped past the vacant land on either side and approached Oberlin Road. A red Mitsubishi Spyder peeled out of DNAY's lot, straightened, and sped after him.

Trevor saw a farm across the empty intersection as he ran the stop sign and turned left onto Oberlin Road. His initial fears about Three Mile Island had been unfounded but could prove useful. If he could reach Three Mile Island, the National Guardsmen providing extra security could back him up.

He passed the gas station convenience store on his right. Not wanting to take 283 East or West, he sped through the red light and crossed Fulling Mill Road. He saw a Ford Ranger crossing the short bridge and coming down the other lane of the two lane road. With the concrete construction barrier to his right and a metal guide rail on his left, he didn't have any room to maneuver. Glass from his rear window exploded across the cargo area and Lyn's body.

Trevor looked in the rearview mirror and saw

Tony propped against the red convertible's front windshield frame, trying to steady his large revolver. They must have used up the SMG ammo breaking out of DNAY. Things weren't as bleak as Trevor had thought, and the Spyder wasn't known for a smooth ride. Maybe Trevor would survive until they ran out of ammunition. If it came down to using his vehicle as a battering ram, he'd match the Highlander against the little Mitsu any day.

Trevor approached the T intersection at the end of Oberlin Road. He wanted to take the left and continue on 441 South toward the power plant. His driver-side mirror shattered. Small shards of glass hit Trevor in the forehead, and one speck landed in his left eye. Trevor jerked the wheel to the right. *Shit! Wrong way!*

He squinted the irritated eye, trying to wash the glass out with blood and tears. He reached up to get it off with his finger. As his finger touched his eye, he realized he wasn't following the windy road and steered left to avoid running up the grass embankment he was rapidly approaching. His finger slid the glass fragment across the white of his eye, slicing it. *Damn that stings!* Now he was heading toward the guide rail across the other lane. He again corrected his course. A bullet punched a hole through the right side of his windshield.

Trevor didn't know how to reach Three Mile Island from this direction. He was approaching a residential area. Children played outside, and adults celebrated a long weekend. He needed to turn around, but if he did it in a busy residential area, he'd endanger innocent people.

He was running out of options. He didn't know how many rounds his enemies still possessed. If he was going to die, he had to call Earl and report as much as possible first. He leaned over to open the glovebox for his cell phone and saw the package on the front seat.

A little farther ahead and to his right, Trevor saw some open fields and the vacant Star Barn. If he could make it that far, he'd have a chance. He placed the bomb between his legs and held the box tightly in place. He flipped open the concealed flap. The agent estimated quickly and set the timer accordingly. He pressed the button to start the countdown.

Trevor ran the stop sign at the intersection and made a hard right. The church set back from the corner remained on his right. Farther ahead was someone's home. *Damn!* Other than a long driveway that led off to the left Trevor saw he didn't have much road ahead. The road he was on came to a dead-end at an embankment under the interstate.

Trevor drove in the center of the two lane road and maintained a constant speed. The red convertible was close now. He checked the countdown on the bomb's display with his good eye. "Special delivery, suckers." He lobbed the package through the open moon roof.

Maintaining his speed, he focused his attention to his rearview mirror and watched the parcel fall. The box burst into a ball of fire as it reached the Mitsu's open cockpit. Tony and the driver were instantly engulfed in flame.

Trevor saw the wooden saw horse and the embankment looming ahead. He hit the brakes but knew he'd never be able to stop in time, even with the ABS. He saw a dirt road behind the Star Barn. He hit the gas and downshifted to second gear for more torque. He swerved hard to the left. The vehicle went up on its right wheels as he accelerated into the turn. The right side of the SUV scraped against the embankment, and the vehicle crashed back down to earth with a jolt. Trevor's head bounced off the roof. He slowed and followed the path around to the other side of the barn and continued through the small field.

The red fireball of a car narrowly missed his SUV as it sped past and crashed into the Star Barn. The dry, rotted timber instantly caught fire. Huge flames climbed the walls and licked at the roof. The structure groaned and sagged then collapsed on the burning Spyder, leaving a huge bonfire to warm the cool day. No one could have survived that. Trevor drove slowly from the field into the street. He stopped the SUV a safe distance from the fire and got out of his vehicle. The people in the house across from him had come out to witness the annihilation of a local landmark.

A man across the street looked at Trevor's battered condition and back to the fire. "Are you okay?"

"I'll be fine, but it's too late to save the Star Barn." Before the family could ask more questions, Trevor got back in his SUV and left the scene.

He returned to the gas station convenience store at the intersection of Fulling Mill and Oberlin Roads. He parked at the furthest pump from the clerk working the cash register, hoping he wouldn't notice the shot out windows and bullet holes marring his SUV. He filled his tank, locked the vehicle out of habit, and entered the store.

The young employee informed him, "Man, you look like shit."

Trevor asked, "Where's your restroom? I need to freshen up." Trevor went in the direction the youth indicated and found the room vacant. He rinsed the glass out of his eye and was grateful that the scratch wasn't deep. The eye would be irritated for awhile, but there should be no permanent damage.

Seeing his reflection in the mirror, Trevor confirmed the clerk's opinion. He did look like shit. Less than a week ago, he was a cocky DOWNS delivery boy. Now, he looked like a decrepit man approaching forty. What did he have to show for it? Enough money to live comfortably, a house, a bullet-ridden SUV, a Porsche, and his pet rabbit. When he died, no one would know how many people he'd saved. He'd leave behind no family, no children, no legacy.

He exited the bathroom. His outward appearance was slightly improved, but his morale was not. Trevor bought a bottle of Pepsi Vanilla and returned to the Highlander. The agent sat in his SUV and called his report in to Earl.

"I'll divert the National Guardsmen from Three Mile Island. They can get the subjects out of the testing chamber. God only knows what those poor souls are thinking by now. We'll have to debrief them. Cover this up. Tell them something went horribly wrong with the experiment. I'll send the PR boys up too. They can put a spin on anything." Earl paused. "You did an incredible job, Trevor."

"I couldn't save Lyn."

"You did everything you could. Take the next two weeks off. You've certainly earned it."

"Yeah." Trevor closed his phone.

He'd barely managed to pull it off this time. Fifty million lives at stake. How many had it cost? What if he wasn't up to his next assignment? What would the death toll be? Two weeks to get his shit back together. His focus. His edge. Then get off the bench and back in the game. Kill or be killed. How much more killing before he lost his sanity and went over the very edge he needed?

He had enough money to resign, throw in the towel. Find a safe, monotonous job. Keep busy. Write his memoirs, package it as fiction, and climb the best sellers' lists. No. Trevor wasn't a quitter. *Two weeks.* He started the engine and began the long drive home.

GO IN PEACE

A week later, Trevor was the solitary mourner at Lynda Flynn's graveside service. He stood near the priest in the church cemetery adjoining the grounds of Macroom Castle. Since Lyn had no living relatives, Trevor had kept his promise to take her back to the castle of her ancestors.

Trevor was depressed, his body numb. His wounds were healing, and he was expected to report for duty in ten days. How would he spend the next nine? Well, there were plenty of pubs in Ireland. If he got bored here, he could go to the pubs in England or Scotland. Was there enough alcohol in the whole United Kingdom to drown his regret?

The elderly priest ended his prayer and commended Lyn's spirit to God. Trevor laid the bouquet on her rosewood casket. "Goodbye, Lyn. I'm sorry. Forgive me."

He turned to Father Murphy and handed him a thick envelope. "This is for your church, the cemetery, and her monument." He shook the priest's cold hand then reached into a pocket and pulled out another envelope. It wasn't as thick as the first one but substantial. "And this is for you, Father. Thank you for taking care of her arrangements. I'm sure it would have meant a lot to her."

The chill in the air seemed to seek a home in Trevor's heart. He'd killed Lyn's murderer, but it wasn't enough to atone for her death. The priest had said something, but Trevor was no longer listening. "Father?"

The old man pointed to the ruins of the nearby castle. "Even hundreds of years later what remains is quite beautiful." Trevor stood and, for the first time, took in the imposing structure on the hill. The sky was a clear blue, and the sun illuminated the ruins from behind. The holy man continued, "So majestic and strong." His frock rippled in the wind, and he removed his glasses to look directly into Trevor's eyes.

Trevor avoided his stare. "You can see the grace in what's left. Must have been incredible when it was new and bustling with life."

Father Murphy replaced his glasses and laid his hands on Trevor's shoulders. "I'd say the same about your lady friend." Trevor looked up and did meet the priest's gaze now. The man's ice-blue eyes were full of compassion. "My son, whatever your burden, the living Lord can free you. Let the dead bury the dead. Would you like me to hear your confession?"

Trevor felt the honest empathy and love this stranger offered. He turned away from the priest and saw a puppy playfully chase a rabbit near the rectory. He considered Karl's desire to be immortalized in history and smirked at the thought that no one would remember the bastard. He contemplated the vestiges of the castle. Their inner strength had allowed them to survive when most of the castle had long since fallen. The priest was right: enjoy life or you might as well be dead.

Trevor recalled what Lyn had said in her living room. *Nothing lasts forever. That's why I enjoy life every day.* He clearly pictured her waving at him outside the DNAY building. He'd cherish the short time they shared. Like a small pebble thrown into a large lake, the ripples peoples' lives made reached far before fading away over time. Trevor smiled.

The cleric saw Trevor's demeanor improve. Trevor now stood at his full height, with a renewed vitality. His brown eyes remained haunted, but they were alive. "Thanks, Father Murphy. I'll skip the confession. You probably don't have that much time to spare anyway."

"Go in peace, my son."

Trevor walked across the holy burial ground and enjoyed the temporary interlude of serenity. It felt good to travel without his guns for once. He could throw his jacket over his shoulder and not reveal the frightening polymer and steel tools of his trade.

In ten days, he'd jump into another assignment with everything he had. He wanted to learn more about the Fundamental Christian Believers Society and destroy them, but Earl couldn't sanction it. Whatever mission Trevor was assigned, it could be his last. He'd just have to do his best.

He left the cemetery and his melancholy behind. Only nine days remained before his next mission. Suddenly, those few days seemed too short a time.